DATE DUE		

F
Mac

300CO00514573L
MacDonald, Betty
Bard.

**Mrs. Piggle-Wiggle's
magic**

**COLEMAN ELEM SCHOOL
SAN RAFAEL,CA**

MRS. PIGGLE-WIGGLE'S MAGIC

Mrs. Piggle-Wiggle's Magic

Betty MacDonald

Pictures by HILARY KNIGHT

HarperCollins*Publishers*

Dedication

To my mother, Sydney Bard, the one most often interrupted, the faithful laugher at "thought you saids," the patient corrector of bad table manners, the rapt listener to long, dull dreams and movie plots, the fairest receiver of tattle tales and eager participant in all timeworn riddles and tricks, I humbly dedicate this book.

Contents

Mrs. Piggle-Wiggle's Magic   *1*

The Thought-You-Saiders Cure   *8*

The Tattletale Cure   *25*

The Bad-Table-Manners Cure   *39*

The Interrupters   *58*

The Heedless Breaker   *70*

The Never-Want-to-Go-to-Schooler   *86*

The Waddle-I-Doers   *107*

MRS. PIGGLE-WIGGLE'S MAGIC

Of course the reason that all the children in our town like Mrs. Piggle-Wiggle is because Mrs. Piggle-Wiggle likes them. Mrs. Piggle-Wiggle likes children, she enjoys talking to them and best of all they do not irritate her.

When Molly O'Toole was looking at the colored pictures in Mrs. Piggle-Wiggle's big dictionary and just happened to be eating a candy cane at the same time and drooled candy cane juice on the colored pictures of gems and then forgot and shut the book so the pages all stuck together, Mrs. Piggle-Wiggle didn't say, "Such a careless little girl can never ever look at the colored pictures in my big dictionary again." Nor did she say, "You must never look at books when you are eating." She said, "Let's see, I think we can steam those pages apart, and then we can

1

wipe the stickiness off with a little soap and water, like this—now see, it's just as good as new. There's nothing as cozy as a piece of candy and a book. Don't look so embarrassed, Molly, I almost drool every time I look at those gems—which one is your favorite?—I think mine is the Lapis Lazuli."

When Dicky Williams, who was showing off for Patsy by riding in his wagon with his eyes shut, crashed through Mrs. Piggle-Wiggle's basement window and landed in the coal bin, Mrs. Piggle-Wiggle laughed so much she had to sit down on the front steps and wipe her eyes with her apron. Dicky was awfully scared and was going to sneak out the basement door and go home, but Mrs. Piggle-Wiggle, still laughing, leaned through the broken window and said, "Hand me the putty knife and that can of putty off the shelf and then go get me that pane of glass leaning against the wall over there by the furnace. Thank you very much. Now watch carefully, Dicky, because putting in window glass is something that every boy should know how to do. Especially boys who ride wagons with their eyes closed."

When Marilyn Matson who was helping Mrs. Piggle-Wiggle serve tea dropped and broke her brown teapot she said, "Well, that's the luckiest thing I've ever known—you didn't get a drop of hot tea on you and you broke that nasty teapot with the leaky spout that I've hated for fifteen years. Tomorrow I'll go to town and buy a new one—I think I'll get pink and I'm going to test the spout before I buy it." "But what about the tea?" said Marilyn, wiping her tears on her sleeve. "Make it in the coffee pot," said Mrs. Piggle-Wiggle, "and we'll call it toffee."

Another nice thing about Mrs. Piggle-Wiggle, when a child makes her a present no matter how splotchy or crooked it might be, she uses it and keeps it where everyone can see it.

Johnny Wilfred made her a vase out of a meat sauce bottle with such a little neck that only flowers with stems like hairs would fit in it. Not only that but he painted it a sort of bilious green and the paint was too thick and ran down the sides in warty lumps. But Mrs. Piggle-Wiggle loves Johnny and she loves the warty vase because Johnny made it for her, and she keeps it on the window sill above the sink with at least one flower, gasping for breath, jammed through its little neck. Every time Johnny comes into her kitchen he points proudly to the vase and says, "Do you see that pretty vase over there on the window sill. Well, I made it for Mrs. Piggle-Wiggle, didn't I, Mrs. Piggle-Wiggle?"

When Susan Gray came staggering over with a plate of the first cookies she had ever made for Mrs. Piggle-Wiggle, Mrs. Piggle-Wiggle didn't take one look at the tannish gray lumps and say, "No Thank You!" She said, "Why, Susan Gray, you smart girl. Eight years old and already making cookies! You're going to make somebody a very fine wife." "Yeah, somebody with good teeth," said Hubert Prentiss who had taken one of the gray lumps and had found that trying to eat it was like biting on a stone. Mrs. Piggle-Wiggle took the cookie away from him and said, "Oh, Hubert, these are special cookies, you dip them in hot tea and then take a bite."

She hurried to the kitchen and made some tea and then

she and Molly and Hubert and Susan sat at the kitchen table and drank tea and gnawed at the stony cookies, which in addition to being hard as rocks, tasted like glue because Susan had put in gravy coloring instead of vanilla. When Molly and Hubert made gagging motions at each other Mrs. Piggle-Wiggle slipped them some ginger cookies under the table and Susan was so proud that she didn't even notice.

Julie Ward knitted Mrs. Piggle-Wiggle a scarf that was about ten yards long and two inches wide and when Mrs. Piggle-Wiggle opened the box she didn't say, "My, Julie, you must have had a giraffe in mind when you made this scarf." Instead she said, "You know Julie, this is much too pretty to wear as a scarf and keep tucked inside my coat. I'm going to wear it as a sash." She took the long, dirty blue, wormy looking scarf and wrapped it around and around her waist and looped the ends over and it did look nice, from a distance. Julie was so proud. She said, "You know, Mrs. Piggle-Wiggle, when I was making that scarf I just thought to myself, 'Now I'll make this longer and then Mrs. Piggle-Wiggle can wear it as a belt too.' " Of course she hadn't really. What actually happened was that she knitted on the scarf every afternoon when she listened to the radio and she just forgot to stop.

Another wonderful trait of Mrs. Piggle-Wiggle's is the interested way she listens to dreams. Now every child in the world loves to tell what he dreams and if the dream doesn't seem to be quite long enough or interesting enough, sometimes some children work in old movies they have seen or stories their Daddies have read to them the night before.

Dream telling is an innocent pastime and very good for the imagination but unfortunately dream telling usually occurs at breakfast, a time when daddies and mothers are slightly irritable and always in a hurry and in no mood for long-drawn-out stories of "and then I was riding on this elephant and two Indians came up and tried to shoot me but then er, uh, uh, uh, I turned into a walnut and dropped on the ground and uh, uh, uh, this—" About this time Mothers say, "Just let the dream go and finish your cereal!" or Brother or Sister will say, "Oh, you're just making that up and anyway it's my turn. Now I dreamed . . ."

Mrs. Piggle-Wiggle not only listens to dreams, she asks about them. Right after school when the children come over to dig for treasure in her back yard (Mr. Piggle-Wiggle was a pirate and when he died he buried his treasure in his back yard) or to have tea or to play dolls, she'll say, "Anybody have any good dreams last night?" and they'll be off.

Once Molly O'Toole dreamed she was a raisin and was eaten by a rat. Johnny Green dreamed that he was a pirate and lived in a whale. Hubert Prentiss dreamed that he was an icicle and could freeze anyone he touched. Susan Gray dreamed that her dolls all came alive. Larry Gray dreamed he was a cowboy and had a white horse. Mary Lou Robertson dreamed that her covers were frosting and woke up with her mouth full of blanket. Kitty Wheeling dreamed that she was a movie star and had a real fur coat. Patsy said that she dreamed that she was an electric toaster and everybody said she was making it up and Patsy cried and Mrs. Piggle-Wiggle said she would help Patsy with her dreams. Some of the children's dreams are so long and dull and full of er—ra and uh—ruh's that Mrs. Piggle-Wiggle finishes them off for them and says, "That was the way it was, wasn't it, Bobby," much to their evident relief.

So you can see that loving children the way she does, Mrs. Piggle-Wiggle just naturally understands them even when they are being very difficult, which is of course why all the mothers in our town call Mrs. Piggle-Wiggle whenever they are having trouble with their children. Mrs. Piggle-Wiggle always knows what to do and then of course she has a big cupboard full of magic powders and pills and appliances to help cure children's bad habits.

THE THOUGHT-YOU-SAIDERS CURE

$\mathcal{M}$r. Burbank absently reached from behind his newspaper for the sugar bowl. His groping fingers hit the toast, the honey comb, the salt cellar and finally found the sugar bowl. His children Darsie, Alison and Bard nudged each other and laughed. Every morning Daddy felt around on the table for the sugar while he read bad news in the newspaper.

One morning the news was so bad and he was so absent-minded he put currant jelly in his coffee. The children were anxious for a repeat performance and hopefully pushed everything but the sugar in the path of his searching hand. This morning as soon as Mr. Burbank had found the sugar he let the paper down with a bang. "The sugar bowl's empty," he said in an aggrieved, hurt way.

8

Mrs. Burbank, who was buttering toast said, "Darsie, run out to the kitchen and fill the sugar bowl, dear. The sugar's in the big red can."

Darsie obediently got up, took the sugar bowl and went out to the kitchen. After a long long time he came back to the breakfast table with a plate of cinnamon rolls.

"What are these for?" his father said. "And where is the sugar?"

"Sugar?" said Darsie. "What about sugar?"

"I told you to fill the sugar bowl," said Mrs. Burbank.

"Oh," said Darsie, "I thought you said, 'Get the cinnamon roll.'"

All three children looked at each other and laughed loudly. Finally Mr. and Mrs. Burbank laughed too. Darsie went out and filled the sugar bowl and Mr. Burbank, after three cups of coffee, missed his bus and decided to walk as far as the school with the children.

Just as they were going out the front door, Alison remembered her arithmetic book and dashed upstairs for it. In a minute she leaned over the bannister and called, "Mother, did you see my arithmetic book?"

Mrs. Burbank said, "What does it look like?"

Alison said, "It's blue and not very thick."

Mrs. Burbank said, "I think it's on the table in the hall."

Alison said, "How did it get out there?"

Mrs. Burbank said, "Out where? I said it's on the table in the hall."

Alison said, "Oh, I thought you said it's out in the stable in a stall." All three children roared with laughter.

Alison found her arithmetic book and they all left the

house laughing and repeating, "Out in the stable in a stall."

Mr. Burbank said, "Come on, come on, we haven't all day." He walked briskly along the street, his footsteps ringing loudly and purposefully in the thin autumn air. The children giggled and jostled along behind him, their progress so uneven and broken by "thought you said" and shrieks of laughter that Mr. Burbank reached the corner first, in fact almost before they had left the yard. He stopped to wait for them and to survey the city spread out below him in the morning sunshine. He was glad he lived on a hill, he was glad he was alive and he was glad he had a little boy nine, a little girl seven and a little boy six.

When the children had caught up with him he said, "Look, children. See how beautiful the city looks from up here. Watch the fog rise over there."

"Where's the dog?" said Bard.

"What dog?" asked Darsie.

"What color are the dog's eyes?" asked Alison.

"What on earth are you talking about?" said Mr. Burbank. "I said, 'Watch the fog rise over there.' "

"Oh," Bard said, "I thought you said, 'Watch the dog's eyes glare.' " All the children laughed and laughed. Mr. Burbank said, "What nonsense," but it was a beautiful morning so he laughed with his lighthearted children.

When they were half way down the next block, the children suddenly stopped stock still in front of a pretty white house and yelled in unison, "Marilyn! Mar-ee-lun! Come on, we'll be late!"

Mr. Burbank said, "That's no way to do. If you want Marilyn, go to the door and ask for her."

The children looked surprised but went obediently up to the door and rang the bell. Marilyn's mother opened the door and said something to the children which seemed to send them into convulsions of mirth. Doubled over with laughter and holding their sides they came down the walk to their father.

"Now what's so funny?" Mr. Burbank asked.

Darsie said, "Marilyn's mother said Marilyn fell in the toaster and is burnt up dead."

Mr. Burbank said, "What did Marilyn's mother really say and why isn't Marilyn going to school."

Alison said, "She said Marilyn fell in her coaster and hurt her head and Darsie thought she said Marilyn fell in the toaster and is burnt up dead." She went into another paroxysm of laughter.

Mr. Burbank didn't laugh. Instead he bent down and examined Darsie's ears which were large and pink and soft and quite clean.

"They *should* work," said Mr. Burbank, looking at the other children's ears. They all seemed quite normal. The children wanted to know what he was doing.

Bard said, "What are you doing that for, Daddy?"

Mr. Burbank said, "I'm trying to decide whether I should get you an ear trumpet."

"Beer crumpet? What's that?" Bard said.

The other children repeated after him, "Beer crumpet? Beer crumpet?" They all laughed but Mr. Burbank, who had had enough. He said, "Come on. I'll supervise a race to school. On your marks, get set, go!"

When Mr. Burbank reached his office the very first thing

he did was to call Mrs. Burbank. He said, "Mary, have our children ever had scarlet fever?"

She said, "Now you know they haven't, Bernard."

"Well," he said, "have they ever had ear infections?"

"Goodness, no," said Mrs. Burbank. "They've never had anything. They are the healthiest children in the neighborhood. What's the matter?"

Mr. Burbank said, "Plenty. They can't any of them hear well. I told them to look at the fog rise and they thought I was talking about dog's eyes. Marilyn's mother said that Marilyn fell off her coaster and hurt her head and they thought she said Marilyn fell in the toaster and was . . ."

". . . Burnt up dead," Mrs. Burbank finished for him. "Bernard, did you ever hear of anyone falling in a toaster? Of course not. There is nothing wrong with our children's ears. It is just that they are going through that awful Thought-You-Said phase."

"Well let's get them out of it," said Mr. Burbank. "They sound like dopes. Dog's eyes, indeed."

Mrs. Burbank said, "Don't worry, dear, I'll take care of it."

As soon as she finished talking to Mr. Burbank, Mrs. Burbank called Marilyn's mother to find out about Marilyn, if she was badly hurt and if there was anything she could do. Marilyn's mother said Marilyn was just fine but the doctor thought she should be quiet for a day or two.

When Mrs. Burbank asked Marilyn's mother if she had ever had any trouble with Thought-You-Said, and told

about the sugar bowl and the cinnamon rolls, the arithmetic book in the stable in the stall, about Marilyn's fall
in the toaster and the dog's eyes, Marilyn's mother said,
"Oh, Mrs. Burbank, I'm so glad you called and told me
all this. You see Marilyn has been doing the same thing all
morning and I was terribly afraid that the blow on her
head had affected her mind. When I asked her if she
wanted crumpets or toast she said, 'Bumped on the nose,
who?' When I asked her if her head pained her she said,
'I thought you said, Is the bed painted yet?' "

Mrs. Burbank said, "I'm going to call up Mrs. Teagle
and see if Terry or Theresa are Thought-You-Saids. She is
such a good manager that if they have Thought-You-Saiditis she's probably thought of a cure." Marilyn's mother
asked Mrs. Burbank to call her back if she got any useful
information and they said goodbye.

Then Mrs. Burbank called Mrs. Teagle. She told her all
about the Thought-You-Saiditis and asked if she had had
any similar experience with Terry or Theresa. Mrs. Teagle
said, "Ohwa, nowa, Mrs. Burrrrbank. Youwa see we have
allaways studied korrect speeeeeech and wea all speak
korrectly. Thee cheeldren alaways pronounce all theirrrr
vowels and all theirrr consonants and therefore we neverrrr
have any trouble understanding each otherrrrr. Perhaps
the trouble lies with you and Mr. Burbank—perrrhaps
you do not speak deestincktly. Perhaps the poor leetle
cheeldrun cannot underrrrstahnd you. I am holding lit-tul
speeeeech clahsses everrrry ahfternoon and eef you and
Mrrrr. Burrrbank are interrrrest-ed I would be glad to
hahve you attend. I wouldn't carrrrre to hahve the cheel-

drun becawse I am afrrrraid they might corrupt my cheel-drun's perrrrfect speeeeeech."

Mrs. Burbank thanked Mrs. Teagle for her kind offer and told her that perhaps she was right. That she and Mr. Burbank would try to speak more distinctly and if things didn't improve within the week they might join the speech classes. Mrs. Teagle said, "Glahd to bee of help annnny tihum, Mrs. Burrbank," and hung up.

That night when Mr. Burbank came home she told him about calling Mrs. Teagle, and told him that she thought that from now on they should both try to speak more carefully so that their poor little children could understand them.

That night at dinner Mr. Burbank announced in a very loud voice, "Pleeeeeese pahssssss the butterrrrrrr!" The children all exchanged glances and whispers, then laughed. The butter remained cool and comfortable on its little plate in front of Darsie.

Mr. Burbank looked accusingly at Mrs. Burbank. She said in a high unnatural voice, "Cheeeldrun, leesten to meee. Pleeeeese pahssss youh fahtherrr the butterrrrrr!"

"Oh," said Darsie, "did you say pass the butter. I thought you said, 'Fleas gasp and mutter.'"

Alison said, "I thought you said, 'He's pa's mother.'"

Bard said, "I thought you said, 'Freeze Pat's brother.'"

Mr. Burbank said in a low grim voice, "I said 'Please pass the butter.'" Darsie passed it to him with a beaming smile.

The next morning after breakfast, Mr. Burbank called from upstairs, "Where's my briefcase, anybody seen my briefcase?"

Alison said, "Whose got a thief's face?"

Darsie said, "Beef paste, what do you want that for?"

Bard said, "Leaf race, I thought he said leaf race." They all laughed loudly and did not look for the briefcase.

They could hear their mother and father banging doors and scuffling around upstairs but they were so busy Thought-You-Saiding they didn't even notice that Bard was standing in front of the briefcase, which was leaning against the radiator in the front hall.

Finally Mr. Burbank came running downstairs, wild-eyed and almost too late for his bus. He called to Mrs. Burbank, "If you find it, dear, bring it right down to the office. I must have it this morning." He slammed the front door and ran like the wind for his bus.

Mrs. Burbank was giving the children their final inspection before school when she saw the briefcase leaning against the wall right behind Bard's fat little legs. She said, "Why children, why didn't you tell Daddy his brief-case was down here. You must have seen it! Now I'll have to make a special trip all the way down to take it to him. Why didn't you tell him?" She looked sternly at her three children.

Alison said, "Briefcase! I didn't know that's what he wanted, I thought he said, 'Thief's face.'"

Darsie said, "I didn't know he wanted his briefcase, I thought he said, 'Beef paste.'"

Bard said, "I thought he said 'leaf race.'"

Mrs. Burbank said, "You know perfectly well that Daddy wouldn't talk about a thief's face, beef paste or leaf races. That's just nonsense and I'm getting good and tired of all this Thought-You-Said business." She sent them off to school with a little push and without a kiss.

But the Thought-You-Saiditis continued all the rest of that week. By Friday morning Mr. and Mrs. Burbank were so irritable they didn't even want to come downstairs and eat breakfast with the Thought-You-Saiders. They tried to solve the problem by not speaking to the children but of course the telephone rang and Mrs. Burbank said to Alison, "Answer the phone" and Alison didn't move and her father said, "ANSWER THE PHONE!" and Alison said, "Oh, answer the phone, I thought you said, 'This ham's got a bone' " and Darsie said, "I thought you said, 'The dancers are home' " and Bard said, "I thought you said, uh, uh, uh, 'The jam's all alone.' " It was the last straw. Mr. Burbank said, "This nonsense has got to stop, now. I'm not going to eat another meal with the Thought-You-Saids."

As soon as the children had left for school and even before she washed the breakfast dishes, Mrs. Burbank decided that she must do something about the Thought-You-Saiders. She poured herself another cup of coffee and sat down at the breakfast table and thought and thought. Ole Boy, the dog, came and sat beside her and she gave him a small piece of ham and stroked his head and wondered and wondered what to do.

She was just going to call Mr. Burbank's mother when the telephone rang again. Mrs. Burbank answered it. It was Mrs. Piggle-Wiggle and she wanted the children to come for tea. Mrs. Burbank said, "Oh, Mrs. Piggle-Wiggle I am so delighted that you called. I was just sitting here at the breakfast table wondering what in the world to do."

And so she told Mrs. Piggle-Wiggle about the Thought-You-Saiders.

Mrs. Piggle-Wiggle said, "There is a regular epidemic of Thought-You-Saiditis all over town. It really is a very harmless disease but can be most annoying to parents, especially when they are trying to hurry. I have suffered with it myself this past week. Put on your shoes is Thought-You-Said sat on a fuse—Get me a tack is Thought-You-Said butter a cracker, and on and on. Fortunately the cure is very simple. I have a magic powder which you sprinkle in the children's ears tonight. It will make their hearing so keen that they'll be able to hear spiders stamping across the floor, leaves crashing to the ground, flowers snapping open their petals and fireflies striking the matches that light their lanterns. I must warn you that tomorrow when the children are wearing the magic hearing powder, you mustn't pop corn, run the vacuum cleaner or serve dry crunchy breakfast foods. The noise would be too painful to them. I'll send the powder over when the children stop by after school. You might lend a little to Marilyn's mother. Goodbye and good luck." Mrs. Piggle-Wiggle hung up the phone.

After school the children came rushing in to deliver the package from Mrs. Piggle-Wiggle and to change their clothes. Mrs. Piggle-Wiggle's package contained a tiny little box of white powder. Mrs. Burbank felt the powder and smelled it—it felt like talcum powder and it smelled like ginger. She put it under the pile of clean handkerchiefs in her handkerchief box. That evening after the children were in bed, she told Mr. Burbank about it. He thought

the magic powder sounded wonderful and decided to try
a little in his own ears.

Mrs. Burbank went up and got the bottle and Mr. Burbank put a pinch in his left ear. Immediately he shouted,
"TURN OFF THAT TERRIBLE RADIO. IT'S KILL-
ING ME." Mrs. Burbank rushed and turned the radio off.
Mr. Burbank said, "It's thundering, we must be going to
have a storm." Mrs. Burbank listened. She couldn't hear
any thunder. She opened the front door and went out and
looked at the sky. It was a clear dark blue and spangled
with stars. The night was as still and quiet as a picture.
Mr. Burbank shouted, "The storm's getting closer. Almost
overhead now!"

Mrs. Burbank came in and closed the door. She said,
"Bernard Burbank, it's a cold, clear, perfectly peaceful
night. There is no thunder."

Mr. Burbank said, "Listen. Don't you hear it. Deafening—that's what it is. Deafening!" Mrs. Burbank listened very carefully. Then she heard from the kitchen a
soft very faint thumping noise. She went out to investigate and found Ole Boy the dog, lying under the kitchen
table scratching and bumping his elbow on the floor. She
gave Ole Boy a dog biscuit and put him out, then she went
back to the living-room and asked Mr. Burbank if the
storm had passed over.

He said, "Do you have to stamp your feet like that?
You certainly must be getting fat, you sound like a coal
truck when you walk."

Mrs. Burbank, who was very slight, looked down at her
soft red house slippers and said, "Bernard, I think you had

better wash that magic powder out of your ear because I'm going to go out right now and get some graham crackers and think of the torture you'll go through if I drop a crumb."

Mr. Burbank said, "Stop shouting!"

Mrs. Burbank said, "I'm whispering, dear," so Mr. Burbank went upstairs to wash out his ear. When he snapped on the light in the bathroom he flinched because it sounded like a pistol shot. When he turned on the faucet it sounded like Niagara Falls and when he accidentally brushed a hairpin off the window sill it sounded like a huge iron chain crashing to the tiled floor.

Mr. Burbank filled the bathroom glass with warm water. He had decided that that would be the best way to wash out the magic powder, and was just about to pour some in his ear when from behind the bathtub he heard the most awful screaming, screeching, whining noise. He straightened up, put down the glass and peered over by the bathtub. He didn't see anything. He bent down over the basin again and picked up the glass. He was just about to pour the warm water in his ear when the horrible, screaming, squealing noise came again, this time right by his head. Mr. Burbank was so scared he dropped the glass, spilled the water and banged his head on the faucet. He looked all around but he couldn't see anything. The noise came again. This time a little fainter and from behind the Venetian blind. He raised the blind and looked carefully. He couldn't see a thing. The terrible noise came again, this time by the mirror; then Mr. Burbank saw what it was. A big mosquito. He grabbed a washcloth and without thinking of his magic hearing, swatted the mosquito. The screams of agony that immediately filled the bathroom were horrible. Mr. Burbank hurriedly turned on the warm water and stuck his ear right under the faucet. Whew, what a relief!

He picked the dead mosquito up by one leg and put it in the wastebasket, then he called to Mrs. Burbank. "Hey, Mary, I'm all right now but I think we'd better go easy with that magic powder in the children's ears. It's awfully strong."

Mrs. Burbank said, "Perhaps you used too much. Here, I'll measure it out. I'll use a toothpick and I'll just put a grain or so in the right ear of each child. Come on now, help me."

They tiptoed into the children's rooms and put a toothpick full of the magic powder in each one's right ear. Even in his sleep Darsie was saying, "Miss Anderson, I didn't hear you say, 'Hand me that ruler'—I thought you said, 'Bananas are cooler.' "

Mr. and Mrs. Burbank looked at their sleeping son and then at each other. "Just wait until tomorrow, Darsie old boy," said Mr. Burbank.

The next morning at seven o'clock, Bard came running into his parents' room and said, "Mother, Daddy, there is a terrible noise in our room. It sounds like sawing." Mr. and Mrs. Burbank got out of bed, put on their robes and went in to investigate. They couldn't hear a thing. Darsie said, "Isn't that a nawful noise, Daddy? Do you think it's a buzz bomb?" Mr. and Mrs. Burbank looked and looked but they couldn't see or hear anything.

Mr. Burbank told the children to get dressed and come down to breakfast. Bard began to cry. He said, "We'll

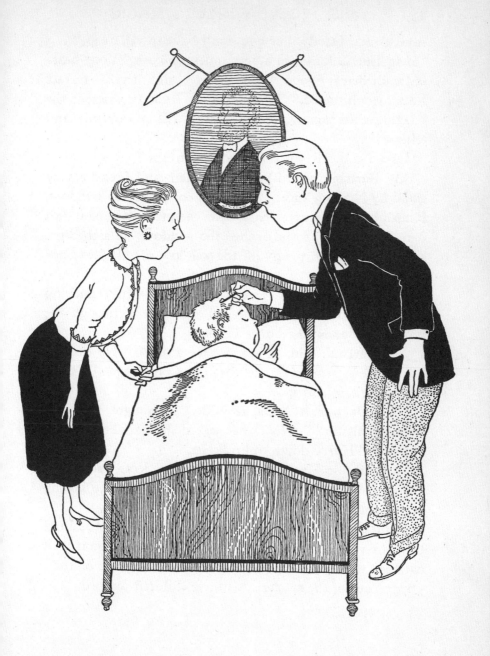

come down, Daddy, but you don't have to yell at us."

Mr. Burbank said in a very quiet whisper, "Your hearing must be very good this morning. I didn't yell—in fact I almost whispered." Then he said, "Exactly where is the buzzing noise coming from, Darsie? Listen carefully and tell me."

Darsie said, "Right there by the curtain."

Mr. Burbank pulled back the curtain and found a very small fly buzzing and buzzing in a corner of the window. Remembering his experience with the mosquito, he didn't dare swat the fly, so he opened the window, unlatched the screen and pushed the fly off the window sill. It flew happily away.

Darsie said, "Daddy, I can't stand this awful crunching noise my shoelaces make when I push them through the holes. It sounds like bones breaking."

Mr. Burbank said, "Here, I have an idea." He tied his handkerchief around Darsie's head like a bandage. "This'll fix it," he said softly.

"Whistle biscuit!" Darsie said. "I thought you said 'Whistle biscuit.'" His father jerked the handkerchief off and said, "Hurry down to breakfast."

At breakfast Alison said, "Oh, Mother, I can't stand the sound of you buttering that toast. It sounds like hoeing on cement."

Bard said, "Hoeing on cement! I thought you said, I thought you said, uh, er ah . . ." He took a spoonful of oatmeal and never finished the sentence. A piece of toast popped out of the toaster. All three children jumped.

Darsie said, "Mother, you should warn us when you're going to make so much noise."

Mrs. Burbank said, "I'm sorry but it didn't seem loud to me. I guess my ears aren't very good."

Alison said, "Come on, boys, let's go to school."

Darsie said, "I thought you said Poison, I mean I thought you said, Poison, I mean . . . Oh, I don't know what I meant."

Alison said, "Ole Boy's breathing so loud I can't hear a thing. And does he have to splash his tongue around in his mouth like that, Mother?"

Mrs. Burbank called Ole Boy and gave him a piece of bacon. He snapped and gulped and all three children jumped and shuddered.

"What a noise," said Alison glaring balefully at poor Ole Boy. "He's just like some terrible kind of a jungle beast."

Mrs. Burbank said, "Come, children, put on your coats and go to school."

Alison said, "Spit on your coats. I thought you said spit on your coats." Nobody laughed.

Darsie said, "Don't talk so loud, Alison, it hurts my ears."

Bard said, "Didn't you hear what Mother said. She didn't say, 'Spit on your coats.' She said, 'Put on your coats.' "

Alison said, "I know it. I can hear. Let's go."

The front door closed quietly and Mrs. Burbank said to her husband, who was groping for the sugar, "That's the first time in five years they haven't banged the front door.

Here's the sugar, dear, and you have four minutes before the next bus."

Just then the front door opened and the three children came crying into the house.

Alison said, "Mother, we just can't stand it. The sidewalk is covered with leaves and when we walk through them the noise is so dreadful we just can't bear it. It sounds like hundreds of giants chopping wood."

Bard said, "It sounds like millions of paper bags."

Darsie said, "It sounds like thousands of houses burning up. Crackle, crackle, crash."

Mrs. Burbank said, "Well, Bernard, I think we'd better wash out their ears and we'll give Mrs. Piggle-Wiggle our heartiest thanks."

Mr. Burbank said, "What's she done wrong?"

"Who?" said Mrs. Burbank.

"Mrs. Piggle-Wiggle," said Mr. Burbank.

"What are you talking about?" said Mrs. Burbank. "I said that we should give Mrs. Piggle-Wiggle our heartiest thanks."

"Oh," said Mr. Burbank. "I thought you said 'Go give Mrs. Piggle-Wiggle your hardest spanks.' "

The children looked disgusted.

THE TATTLETALE CURE

It was a cold snowy day. Mrs. Hamilton gave the hot cocoa a little stir and then went to the kitchen window to see if the children were coming. It was ten minutes past three and almost time for them. Mrs. Hamilton fixed a plate of sugar cookies and got out two big shiny red apples. Then just as the children rounded the corner she poured the hot, fragrant cocoa.

Wendy and Timmy came stamping up on the back porch and Mrs. Hamilton helped them off with their galoshes, brushed off some of the snow and hurried them into the nice warm kitchen.

"And how was school?" she asked Wendy as she helped her off with her coat and leggings.

Wendy said, "Well, I hate everybody at school and everybody at school hates me."

Mrs. Hamilton was shocked. Wendy was nine years old. She had nice fat pigtails, shiny brown bangs, sparkling brown eyes and pink cheeks. Mrs. Hamilton didn't see how anyone could hate her. She said, "Why Wendy, that's dreadful, dear. Why does everyone hate you?"

Wendy said, "I don't know. They just do. And I don't care because I hate everybody." She sat down at the kitchen table and took a bite of sugar cookie.

Timmy, who was seven, was sitting on the floor taking off his leggings. His mother said, "Here, Timmy, let me help you."

Timmy said, "No thanks. I can do it myself. You want to know why everybody hates Wendy—it's because she's such an old tattletale. She tells the teacher on everybody. I hate her too."

Mrs. Hamilton said, "Why, Wendy Hamilton. Do **you** tell on people?"

Wendy said with evident pride, "Uh, huh. I tell Miss Worthington every time anybody whispers or cheats or writes notes. I even told her when Jimmy Murton sucked his paintbrush today. We're not supposed to suck our paintbrushes; we're supposed to use our fingers to make points." She took a little sip of her cocoa and wiped her lips daintily. Wendy was very pleased with herself.

Mrs. Hamilton wasn't pleased with her. She said, "Wendy Hamilton, I think that's horrid. Telling the teacher about a little thing like sucking a paintbrush."

Timmy said, "Oh, she's always in there tattling. She's so busy spying and tattling she doesn't even have time to play."

Wendy said, "You better be careful, Mr. Timothy

Hamilton, or I'll tell Mother that you haven't brushed your teeth for five nights and you gave your liver to Spot last Wednesday and you spent some of your Sunday School money on candy and last night you read in bed with a flashlight."

Timmy said, "Yeah, and this morning you put the rest of your toast in the silverware drawer, you spilled Spot's water and didn't wipe it up, and you ate half the candy I bought with my Sunday School money."

Wendy, quite red in the face, said, "Oh, bah, bah, bah, to you, you old crumpet."

"Bah, bah, bah, yourself, old dog eyes," Timmy said.

Wendy said, "Motherrrrrrrr, he calls me dog eyes all the time. He says that only dogs have brown eyes."

Mrs. Hamilton said, "Wendy, change your school clothes and then go in and start your practising. Timmy, change your school clothes and then go down in the basement and put away all of Daddy's tools that you got out last night. I must say, you're both so disagreeable I'm sorry you came home from school and spoiled my nice peaceful afternoon."

Mrs. Hamilton went up to her sewing-room and closed the door. There was a nice little fire in the grate and it was very cozy in there with the radio playing softly, big snow-flakes drifting down past the window and no sounds of quarreling from downstairs. Mrs. Hamilton was letting down the hems of Wendy's summer dresses and as she sewed she thought about the tattling and wondered why Wendy had turned into such a horrible little prig. Tattling was a loathsome disease and she was afraid that Timmy was catching it too.

While Mrs. Hamilton sewed and worried, the snow piled

up in fluffy white heaps on the window sills, the coals hummed and blazed in the grate and from downstairs came "da, daa, duh, duh, da, daa, duh, duh, daa, daa, daa, daa, daa, daaaa, duh, duh . . ." as Wendy practised *The Happy Farmer*.

Mrs. Hamilton had just reached the stage where she was thinking, "Oh, well, it will all straighten out. Wendy is just going through a phase," when the practising suddenly stopped, the sewing-room door was thrown dramatically open and Wendy announced, "I think you should know that Timmy is just sitting on the basement stairs looking at a book and when I told him to do his work he said, 'Oh, go bang on the piano, Dog Eyes.' "

Mrs. Hamilton said, "I didn't tell you to check up on Timmy. I told you to do your practising."

Wendy said, "If I don't see that Timmy does his work, who's going to? You just sit up here and sew with the door closed."

Mrs. Hamilton said, "When I need your help, Wendy, I'll ask for it. Now go downstairs and finish your practising." Wendy turned and flounced down the stairs.

Mrs. Hamilton got up and closed the sewing-room door. Again everything was peaceful. *The Happy Farmer* was thumped out indignantly on the piano and from the basement there was silence. This lasted exactly ten minutes. Then the sewing-room door was again thrown open to reveal both Wendy and Timmy jostling for position and tattling at the top of their lungs. "She's just an old spy . . . He's not doing a thing but reading . . . Nobody likes her and that includes me . . . He's the one that ate all those ginger snaps last winter . . . If you want to know what happened to that old fountain pen that Mrs. Wentworth left here three years ago, Wendy took it to school and Marty Phillips stepped on it and ... Timmy owes thirteen cents on his library books and he can't find his card ... He called me Dog Eyes right in front of everybody at recess ... She broke my kaleidoscope ... He spilled ink in my desk drawer ... She hit me ... He teases me ..."

Mrs. Hamilton marched them to their rooms and closed the doors. "You're to be perfectly quiet and stay in your rooms until dinner time." With a sigh she went downstairs to start dinner. She had just put the teakettle on when the telephone rang. "Hello," said Mrs. Hamilton.

"Hello," said Mrs. Piggle-Wiggle. "I've just baked gingerbread and I wondered if Timmy and Wendy wouldn't like some. Molly O'Toole is making the tea and Kitty Wheeling is setting the table."

Mrs. Hamilton said, "Oh, that's very kind of you, Mrs. Piggle-Wiggle, but Wendy and Timmy are being so naughty I have sent them to their rooms to stay until dinner time."

Mrs. Piggle-Wiggle said, "Oh, I'm sorry to hear that. What seems to be the trouble?"

"Tattling," said Mrs. Hamilton. "Wendy came home this afternoon and told me that she tells the teacher on everyone in school. She also tattles on Timmy and Timmy tattles on her. I'm really terribly distressed. I simply despise tattletales."

"Oh, so do I," said Mrs. Piggle-Wiggle, "but Tattletale-itis is certainly a common ailment among children. 'Johnny said Bah, bah, bah, and I said Boo, boo, boo and Johnny said You're an old ugh and I said Is that so then you are too and he said Hah, hah, aha . . ." Mrs. Piggle-Wiggle laughed. She said, "I have listened to every kind of tattling there is. I have heard the sneaks, the teacher's pets, the cry-babies, the mama's boys, the bosses, the little prissies, the whiners, every variety of tattletale and I know that tattle-tales are really unhappy children."

Mrs. Hamilton said, "Wendy told me this afternoon that everybody at school hates her but she doesn't care be-cause she hates everybody at school."

"At present that is only temporary," said Mrs. Piggle-Wiggle. "But I do think we should start the tattletale cure right away. I have some marvellous medicine which I'll send over with Molly O'Toole on her way home. The pills look and taste just like licorice drops but the effect is quite remarkable. Let me see, today is Thursday. Better not give the medicine to Wendy and Timmy until Friday night. Give them each a pill Friday night and another one on Saturday. Call me Sunday night and let me know how things are. Oh, by the way, I wouldn't plan on having any company over the week-end—the tattletaleitis cure is rather startling. Goodbye. Give my love to Wendy and Timmy."

There was a little click as Mrs. Piggle-Wiggle hung up the phone.

Mrs. Hamilton sat and looked at the telephone for a few minutes. "Little Black pills—remarkable effect. I wonder what they are? I wonder what they do?"

About five-thirty, Molly O'Toole, all frosted with snow and starry-eyed from eating hot gingerbread, rang the doorbell and handed Mrs. Hamilton a small package.

"A present from Mrs. Piggle-Wiggle," Molly said.

"Mrs. Piggle-Wiggle said to tell Wendy and Timmy that she's baking gingerbread next Thursday and for them to be sure and be there."

Mrs. Hamilton asked her to come in but she said no she had to go home and set the table and she turned and skipped off into the snowy winter evening.

Mrs. Hamilton went into the kitchen and undid Mrs. Piggle-Wiggle's package. There was a small black box marked CURE FOR TATTLETALEITIS. Inside the box was a small black bottle. Inside the bottle were four black pills. Mrs. Hamilton examined the pills very carefully. They looked and smelled just like licorice drops but she was sure they weren't licorice drops because Mrs. Piggle-Wiggle had said they were magic and they undoubtedly were. She put the pills back in the bottle, put the bottle back in the box and put the box on the top shelf of the spice cupboard by the stove. Somehow or other just seeing that box marked CURE FOR TATTLETALEITIS made her feel better. She hummed as she got dinner and set the table and when Mr. Hamilton came home he looked so tired that she didn't mention her trouble of the afternoon. Instead she waited until dinner was on the table before calling the children and then she pretended not to notice their tight little buttonhole mouths and flashing eyes.

When Timmy put almost a half a baked potato in his mouth and Wendy started to tattle about it, Mrs. Hamilton quickly sent her to the kitchen for the pepper grinder. When Wendy gulped her milk and Timmy opened his mouth to tattle, Mrs. Hamilton said, "Oh, look at poor Spotty, he's so hungry he has tears in his eyes." By constant maneuvering, dinner was kept tattle free.

But the next morning and afternoon were horrible. The children quarreled and tattled from the moment they got up until they went to bed. Mrs. Hamilton closed her ears and thought of the little black pills. But Mr. Hamilton finally gave Wendy and Timmy each a spanking and told them that they could tattle to each other about him. Just before they went to sleep and when they had stopped crying sufficiently so that she was sure they wouldn't choke, Mrs. Hamilton gave them each one of the licorice drops. She could hardly wait until morning to see what the magic medicine would do.

The next morning it was still snowing and the children slept late. Wendy was the first downstairs. She came shuffling into the kitchen looking like a cross between a scarecrow and a windmill. She had put on an old faded very small pair of summer shorts, a thin raggedy T-shirt and some old white sandals of her mother's. She hadn't washed her face and she had slept wrong on her braids so that one pointed north and one pointed south. Her eyes were all squinty and sleepy.

Mrs. Hamilton said, "Wendy Hamilton, there is a blizzard blizzing outside and here you come downstairs in all your old summer clothes. Go up and put on your blue jeans and a sweater, wash your face and brush your teeth and bring me the hairbrush." Wendy gave her mother a baleful look and went shuffling back upstairs.

Then Timmy came down. He had on his jeans and a sweater but when his mother went to roll up his sleeves to see if he had washed, she found that he had on his pajamas and not only that but under his pajamas he had on his underwear. As Mrs. Hamilton sent him back upstairs to change, she wondered fearfully if the strange outfits her children had put on had anything to do with the magic pills. She certainly hoped not. It was bad enough to have two little tattletales but to have tattletales who slept in their underwear and wore their pajamas in the daytime and wore summer clothes in the middle of winter, was well-nigh unbearable.

As Mrs. Hamilton took up the children's oatmeal and poured their milk, she glanced fearfully toward the back stairs. How would they look this time and what had the magic pills done to them. In no time at all she had her answer. First she heard shrill fighting voices, quick chasing footsteps, slaps and yelps and then racing down the stairs came the tattlers, each redfaced and anxious to tell first.

"Motherrrrrrrrrrrr," said Wendy as she slid through the kitchen door. "Motherrrrrrr, Timmy—" but instead of the long tattletale she intended, out of Wendy's mouth came a big puff of black smoke. The puff of smoke was shaped like a little black cloud except that hanging fom the bottom of it were four little black tails. Little black tattletales. The black cloud rose to the ceiling and stuck—the four little tails swayed gently back and forth.

Timmy said, "My Gosh, did you see that. Smoke came out of Wendy's mouth. Say, Mother, I bet ole Wendy's been—" but instead of saying "smoking" as he intended, a big puff of black smoke came out of his mouth. It too was a little black cloud but it had only one tail hanging from it because he had only intended to tattle about one thing. Timmy and Wendy stood with their mouths open staring at the ceiling.

Mrs. Hamilton said, "Well, I've always wondered what

a tattletale looks like, now I know. Ugh, what ugly things!" Wendy and Timmy didn't say anything. They looked at the ceiling, then at each other and then back at the ceiling. Finally they sat down to breakfast.

After breakfast it was still snowing hard but Wendy and Timmy said they were going out to shovel the walks. They put on their leggings, coats, caps and mittens without a word but they couldn't decide whose galoshes were whose and they began jerking them back and forth and pushing and shoving and finally were just going to yell for Mrs. Hamilton to tattle when out of their open mouths came two huge rolls of black smoke each with a long black tattle-tale suspended from it. The two new tattletales soared slowly upwards and stuck to the ceiling not far from the first two.

Wendy said, "What if that happened in school?"

Timmy said, "Boy, the kids would sure be surprised. I can just hear ole Miss Harkness. She'd say, 'Timothy Hamilton, you have been SMOKING!' "

Wendy said, "I don't think I'd like to have that happen in school. All the children would laugh at me. Hey, these are your galoshes. I can tell because they are a teensy bit littler than mine."

They put on their galoshes and went quietly out to shovel the walks.

Every once in a while Mrs. Hamilton peered out at them. She wondered what would happen to the black tattletales outside. Would they float clear up to the sky or would they hang just above the head of the tattler. About noon Mrs. Hamilton found out. The children had finished the walks and were building a snowman. Wendy, who was the

tallest, was putting on the head when she slipped and fell against the snowman and knocked him over. Timmy was furious. He thought Wendy had deliberately knocked over the snowman and he ran and pounded on the front door and yelled for his mother—to tattle.

When Mrs. Hamilton opened the front door Timmy opened his mouth and out came a big black puff of smoke with a tattletale hanging from it. The smoke rose slowly until it was about four feet above Timmy's head. There it stayed. When he walked it moved with him. Timmy took his shovel and tried to bat the tattletale but the shovel went right through it and all it did was to make the tail swing a little.

Wendy thought it was very funny. She said, "I'm going to get Molly and Dick and Hubert and Patsy so they can all see what an old tattletale you are."

Timmy said, "You do and I'll wash your face with soap, ole Dog Eyes."

Wendy said, "You just try it, and Mother said you weren't to call me Dog Eyes. I'm going to tell Mother. She said she'd punish you if you called me Dog Eyes. Motherrrrrrr!"

Out of Wendy's mouth came a big puff of black smoke with a big black tail hanging from it. It floated up until it was about four feet over Wendy's head and there it stayed. Wendy said, "Come on, Timmy, let's go in the house. What if the postman should see those old black things." They put away their shovels and went in the house. The black tattletales followed them in and floated up to the kitchen ceiling to join the other tattletales.

Once during the afternoon a strange thing happened.

Wendy and Timmy were coloring at the kitchen table and Timmy joggled Wendy's elbow and Wendy was just going to tattle on Timmy when suddenly remembering the ugly black tattletales, she looked up at the ceiling and swallowed her tattling. As the tattletale went back down her throat Wendy noticed that one of the ugly black clouds shriveled up and disappeared.

A few minutes later Wendy broke Timmy's red crayon and he started to get up to tattle when he happened to look up at the ceiling. Seeing all the ugly black tattletales made him decide that perhaps Wendy didn't mean to break his red crayon so he swallowed his tattletale and sat down again. Immediately another black cloud shriveled up and disappeared from the ceiling.

By the time Mr. Hamilton came home there were only two left. The one with the four tails and the biggest one with one tail. Mr. Hamilton took one look at the ceiling and said, "Good Heavens, did the oil burner blow up?"

Mrs. Hamilton said, "Come in the living-room a minute, Charles, I want to talk to you."

In a few minutes Mr. Hamilton came out to the kitchen with a golf club with which he poked and poked at the tattletales. It didn't do any good. The golf club went right through them but they didn't move or change shape.

During dinner the children were surprisingly quiet and surprisingly pleasant. In fact, there wasn't a cross word spoken the entire evening. When they went to bed Mrs. Hamilton gave them the last of the pills but she didn't really feel that it was necessary.

After the children were in bed, Mr. Hamilton got up on the kitchen stool and tried to pull down the tattletales.

It was like trying to pull down smoke. He finally gave up. He said, "That's the darnedest thing I've ever seen."

Mrs. Hamilton said, "I think they're beautiful."

On Sunday, Wendy made one more tattletale and Timmy shriveled his last old one. Sunday night Mrs. Hamilton called Mrs. Piggle-Wiggle. She told her everything that had happened and asked her if she thought the children were cured. Mrs. Piggle-Wiggle said that she was sure they were cured but that the important thing was for Mrs. Hamilton never to tell the children about the magic medicine in case she ever had to use it again.

Monday morning all the tattletales were gone from the kitchen ceiling, and if Wendy and Timmy had known it they could have tattled to their hearts' content and no smoke would have come out of their mouths because they hadn't taken any magic medicine the night before. But they didn't know it and every time they started to tattle they would gulp and look guiltily at the ceiling.

Monday afternoon Wendy came home from school and said that everyone in school liked her and she liked everybody. Timmy didn't say anything. He had a black eye and a skinned nose but he didn't say a word. He and Wendy laughed and talked as they drank their cocoa but they kept their eyes on the ceiling.

THE BAD-TABLE-MANNERS CURE

"Slop, slurp, gulp, bang," Christopher Brown was through with his milk. His mother was in the pantry polishing silver but she didn't have to go into the kitchen to see that Christopher was through eating. She could tell because the loud noises had stopped. Mrs. Brown was terribly ashamed of Christopher's table manners and she talked and talked and talked and talked and talked and talked, but so far it hadn't done a speck of good.

Christopher was ten years old and a very nice little boy in other ways. He had red hair, he was a fine baseball player, he was a good sport, he got excellent grades in school and he kept his room reasonably neat, but he certainly had horrible table manners. No, that isn't right—he really had no table manners at all. He ate just like an animal. A starving, wild animal.

Mr. and Mrs. Brown had gradually become used to Christopher's table manners. Of course they made him eat in the kitchen, but what worried Mrs. Brown so terribly was that some day one of Christopher's friends would invite him to dinner. Not just a children's party. Chris had been to lots of those and he was so much fun and so good at the games that the children didn't care if he ate like a starving animal. No, Mrs. Brown was afraid he'd be asked to stay all night or to visit in another town or to go to the country with some of his friends' families. How dreadful it would be when Christopher took his first bite and began to chew!

Christopher chewed with his mouth open so that you could see all the food as he rinsed it around in his mouth. Also he smacked his lips so loud it sounded like someone slapping their hands on water; he gulped when he swallowed; he washed food down with milk; he made enormous piles of meat, potatoes, peas, carrots and gravy on his fork and then thrust the fork so far down his throat you could hardly see the handle; he used his thumb to assemble big fork loads; he propped his knife and fork against his plate with the handles on the table; he buttered whole slices of bread on his hand; he chopped and smashed and mixed his food until his dinner looked like dog food; he picked up his soup bowl and held it just under his chin while he slurped his soup; he talked while he was chewing; he gestured with a fork full of food so that bits of food shot around the room like stones from a slingshot. I could go on indefinitely about Christopher's table manners but I think I've told enough to show you that having Christopher sitting beside you at the table was almost exactly like eating next to a wolf. Watching him eat was certainly not a sight to whet the appetite.

Mrs. Brown rubbed polish on the silver and thought about Christopher's table manners and was sad. "There should be a school for table manners," she said to herself, "and attendance should be compulsory."

The telephone rang. It was Mrs. Thompson, Dick's mother. She said, "I'm having a few of Dick's friends over for dinner a week from Saturday. My brother Charles, the big game hunter, is going to visit us for a few days and I thought it would be so nice if some of Dick's friends could meet Charles and see his movies of hunting lions and tigers in Africa. I'm just asking Christopher, Hubert Prentiss and Larry Gray because there will be twelve grown-ups too."

Mrs. Brown thanked Mrs. Thompson, said that she knew Christopher would be delighted and then went out and made herself a big pot of black coffee. Her hands shook when she poured the first cup. Twelve grown-ups and Mrs. Thompson's famous brother Charles, all sitting at the table with Christopher. Mrs. Brown couldn't bear even to think about it. "Oh, what will I do? What will I do?" she said. She would give Christopher a good talking to and he would be very nice and pleasant and agree to everything she said and really try to have better manners for a meal or two. Then back he'd go, slurp, splash, smack, crunch, choke, gurgle, gulp, bang! Mrs. Brown shuddered.

She called her friend Mrs. Penzil. She said, "Mrs. Penzil, I'm not going to beat around the bush. My son Christopher has the worst table manners in the whole world, and I don't know how to cure them. Do Percy, Pamela and

Potter have nice table manners?"

Mrs. Penzil said, "Why I never noticed, Mrs. Brown. You see Percy, Pamela and Potter have always been allowed to make their own decisions about everything. As soon as they were born we gave them free rein and actually I haven't seen them eat for several years."

"What do they live on?" Mrs. Brown asked. "Oh, they eat," said Mrs. Penzil, "but only when the need for food occurs to them. Now Potter eats nothing but peanut butter and poppy seeds, and he always eats at night. He says that eating during the day is much too common a practice and should be stopped. Pamela eats nothing but weenies and bananas. She does her own shopping and peels the bananas herself which I think is very progressive for a child of seven years."

"I don't," said Mrs. Brown crossly. "I think it's dreadful to let a child live on weenies and bananas. What does Percy eat?"

"Percy? Now let me see," said Mrs. Penzil. "Oh, yes, Percy. Why Percy eats anything. He is most co-operative. Just give him cookies, candy, marshmallows, cake, ice cream and root beer and you don't have to worry about Percy. He's a fine boy."

Mrs. Brown said, "Well, Mrs. Penzil, I guess everyone has their problems. You have cheered me up a lot and I do hope you know a good doctor. You are going to need one."

Mrs. Penzil said, "Oh, I think not. Both Mr. Penzil and I were brought up the same way and we're both terribly happy. Mr. Penzil never eats anything but kippered salmon and Grapenuts and I never eat . . ."

Mrs. Brown hung up the phone. "Kippered salmon and Grapenuts—ugh."

She called Mrs. Piggle-Wiggle and told her the whole problem. She didn't leave out a thing when she described the way Christopher ate and when she told about the dinner party he had been invited to and how ashamed she was going to be, she got tears in her eyes.

Mrs. Piggle-Wiggle said, "Now, Mrs. Brown, don't worry so. Christopher is such a darling boy and I know how to cure him. It's going to take co-operation on your part and it may be a little inconvenient, but I have the cure. I'm going to lend you Lester."

"Lester?" said Mrs. Brown. "Who is he?"

"He is a pig," said Mrs. Piggle-Wiggle.

"Oh, no!" said Mrs. Brown. "Not a pig! I have no place to keep a pig and this is a restricted neighborhood."

"Just a minute," said Mrs. Piggle-Wiggle. "Lester is absolutely no trouble. He has beautiful manners, is very quiet and sleeps in the basement. So nobody in the neighborhood need know about him."

"But where shall I put his trough?" said Mrs. Brown.

"Oh, Lester doesn't use a trough," said Mrs. Piggle-Wiggle. "That's the whole point. Lester has the most beautiful table manners you have ever seen, and I want him to eat at the kitchen table with Christopher. You'll be very surprised. Lester will teach Christopher how to eat."

"But it sounds fantastic!" said Mrs. Brown.

"I know," said Mrs. Piggle-Wiggle. "Every mother I send Lester to has the same feeling. But let me tell you that once you have had Lester in your house, you won't want to let him come home to me. I always have that trouble. Everybody adores Lester and wants to keep him. Oh, by the way, he likes to sleep on a clean blanket on the basement floor. Also he likes to have the basement door left open so he can go out for his exercise after dark and when the neighbors are asleep. Have Christopher stop by after school and I'll send Lester over. Mrs. Martin just returned him this morning."

"But what does he eat?" said Mrs. Brown.

"Exactly what Christopher does, except much larger portions. Oh, yes, I almost forgot. Lester is very fond of coffee. He takes cream and sugar and he often drinks as many as five cups at a meal. Now don't worry, Mrs. Brown. Fix Lester a nice bed on a clean blanket by the furnace and I'm sure he'll solve all your problems. Goodbye."

Mrs. Brown went up and got a clean blue blanket out of the guest-room closet and with many misgivings unfolded it and put it on the floor beside the furnace in the basement. She looked at the clock. She had ten minutes before she could expect Christopher. She made some cocoa with whipped cream, fixed two plates of ginger cookies, one much larger than the other, and polished two large red apples. She got out spoons and napkins and then remembering what Mrs. Piggle-Wiggle had said about Lester's manners, she took two of her good linen doilies and put them on the kitchen table.

At exactly three-thirty there was a knock at the back door and there stood Christopher, who usually never knocked, and a large white pig. Christopher said, "Mother, this is Lester and we got to keep him. Oh, he's fun! He's so smart he knows everything, don't you, old boy?"

Mrs. Brown said, "Come in, Christopher and Lester, I have some cocoa for you."

Christopher said, "Oh, boy," dashed over to the table and began gulping his cocoa. Lester walked daintily into the kitchen, closed the door carefully behind him, climbed up and sat down across the table from Christopher. Christopher was jamming his mouth full of cookie and washing it down with cocoa. Lester looked at him, then took one cookie carefully between the split in his front hoof and ate it very slowly and with tiny bites. He picked his cocoa cup up with his hoof and after one small sip put it carefully down, while he patted his snout with his napkin.

Christopher stopped eating, or at least stopped chewing, to watch Lester eat. Christopher's mouth was open but full, he had whipped cream on his upper lip and crumbs on his chin. Lester reached across the table and gently closed Christopher's mouth. Then he wiped the whipped cream off his upper lip and the crumbs off his chin.

Christopher was delighted. He said, with his mouth full, "Gosh, you're smart, Lester."

Lester put his hoof across his lips and pointed to Christopher's full cheeks to indicate, "No talking with a full mouth."

Christopher looked up at his Mother. "Isn't he smart, Mother? Isn't Lester wonderful?"

Lester looked over at Mrs. Brown and she was sure he winked at her.

It usually took Christopher about three and a quarter minutes to gag down his cookies and cocoa. This day, either because of the excitement of having Lester with him or perhaps because of the good example set by Lester, Christopher was still eating at four o'clock. Mrs. Brown came downstairs to clear up the cocoa things and was most surprised to find that Christopher had only just finished and Lester was but half way through. Mrs. Brown asked Lester if he'd care for some more cocoa and he nodded his head and handed her his cocoa cup.

Christopher said that he didn't care for any more and began eating his apple—crash, crunch, smash, gulp. Lester reached across the table and took the apple away from him, got down off his chair, went over to a drawer in the kitchen, took a knife and cut Christopher's apple into small sections, cored each section, put them on the empty cookie plate and handed the plate to Christopher. Christopher put a whole section of apple in his mouth. Lester shook his head at him, reached over and took one of the sections and took one very small bite. Chris gulped down the first section and took another, but this time, instead of stuffing it all in his mouth, he took one small bite. Lester nodded approvingly at him.

At four-thirty both Lester and Christopher had finished their cocoa and apples and Christopher took Lester down to the basement to show him his bed. Lester looked carefully around the furnace room, straightened out several wrinkles in the blue guest-room blanket, then nodded at Christopher to show him the bed was all right. They went into the game room. There was a red tennis ball on the floor. Lester picked it up and threw it at Chris. Chris caught it and threw it back. Lester caught it neatly in his mouth, then took it out with his hoofs and threw it at Chris. They played ball until it was time for the mystery

cowboy radio programs that Christopher listened to every evening.

He said to Lester, "Gee, Lester, I hope you don't mind but I always listen to a bunch of keen radio programs at five o'clock. Of course, if you'd rather play ball, I don't have to."

Lester shook his head, turned and pointed to the fire-place, where a nice little fire was laid.

Christopher said, "Do you want me to light the fire, Lester, do you?"

Lester nodded. Christopher struck a match and lit the paper. Lester stretched out on the hearth rug and closed his eyes. Christopher crouched by the radio and listened to his programs. It was very peaceful.

When Mr. Brown came home from work, Mrs. Brown told him about the invitation to dinner to meet Mrs. Thompson's famous brother, Charles, about Mrs. Piggle-Wiggle and about Lester. Mr. Brown was most skeptical about Lester being able to teach Christopher table manners. "Talk about the blind leading the blind," he said and laughed loudly.

Mrs. Brown said, "Hush, Phillip, Lester's right down in the basement and really he has the most beautiful table manners I've ever seen."

Mr. Brown said, "Guess I'll go down and have a look at Lester."

He went down the basement stairs whistling, "Who's afraid of the big, bad wolf?"

Mrs. Brown groaned. Mr. Brown looked first in the woodroom; no Lester. Then he looked in the furnace room. He saw the blue guest-room blanket lying on the floor so he picked it up, shook it, took it into the laundry and stuffed it in the laundry chute. He went around the laundry peering under the washing machine, laundry tubs and ironing board saying, "Oink, oink, oink." He got no response. He noticed that the basement door was open a little so he closed and locked it, muttering about burglars and carelessness.

Then hearing the radio from the game room he decided to go in and ask Christopher where he kept his pig. He was certainly surprised to see Lester lying on the hearth rug in front of a crackling fire apparently listening to the radio. He said, "So this is Lester. Oink, oink, oink!"

Lester opened his eyes and gave him a cold look, then seeing that it was Mr. Brown he jumped to his feet and held out his hoof.

"Well, I'll be darned!" said Mr. Brown, shaking hands and beaming.

Christopher said, "Boy, isn't Lester smart, Daddy? Isn't he?"

Mr. Brown said, "I always said that you can teach a pig anything. Pigs are the smartest animals there are." Lester still looked coldly at him. He hadn't forgiven him for the Oink, oink, oink business. Mr. Brown bent over and began scratching Lester behind the ears. Lester gently but firmly pushed his hand away, then went over and lay down again by the fire. Mr. Brown, slightly red in the face, said, "Well, I guess I'd better see how dinner is coming along."

Christopher said, "Just a minute, Daddy, I want to show you how keen Lester plays ball. Come on, Lester old boy. Let's play a game." He picked up the red tennis ball and Lester rather unwillingly got to his feet. Christopher threw him the ball and he caught it in his mouth and threw it back. Christopher threw it again and Lester caught it but this time Lester threw it to Mr. Brown. Mr. Brown was so surprised he almost missed but you could tell he was pleased because he kept looking at Lester and smiling. They played three-cornered catch until Mrs. Brown called to say dinner was ready and to tell Christopher to wash his hands.

There was a small lavatory off the game room and Christopher rushed in and in his usual way, wet his hands, splashed a little water on his face and was going to wipe all the dirt off on the towel, when Lester, who had followed him in, took the towel away from him and put it back on the towel rack; put the stopper in the basin, filled it to the brim with hot water and began washing his own face and hoofs thoroughly and with lots of soap. When he had finished he let the water out of the basin and filled it up with fresh hot water for Christopher.

While Lester dried his nice clean face and hoofs, Christopher washed, thoroughly and with lots of soap. While he dried his face and hands, Lester took the hairbrush and dampened and smoothed the bristles on his neck and around his ears. Christopher watched him, then dampened and brushed his hair too. Then they went up to dinner.

Unfortunately Mrs. Brown, forgetting about Lester, had spareribs for dinner. They were crisp and brown and Mr. Brown gave Lester an extra large helping. Lester sat down at the table, smiled because everything looked and smelled so delicious, unfolded his napkin, took a sip of milk, then cut off a small piece of the sparerib. He put it in his mouth, began to chew, then turned terribly pale and pushed his plate away.

Christopher watched him anxiously. "Gosh, Lester, what's the matter? Don't you like spareribs?"

Lester took his spareribs and put them on Christopher's plate.

Christopher said, "Lester, I'll go tell Mother you don't like spareribs. She'll fry you some eggs or something. That's what she does for Daddy when he doesn't like something." He started to get down from his chair. Lester reached over and took hold of his shoulder. He shook his head sternly, pointed to Christopher's dinner, and by chewing motions indicated that Christopher was to continue with his dinner.

Lester had two helpings of dressing, sweet potatoes and string beans. He also ate his salad, two dishes of peaches, two pieces of applesauce cake and drank four cups of coffee. Christopher ate all his dinner and with much less noise than usual. He even asked Lester if it was all right to pick his sparerib bones up in his fingers.

After dinner he and Christopher and Mr. Brown played ball for a while. Then it was time for Chris to go to bed. He and Mr. Brown said goodnight to Lester and went upstairs.

Lester went in to his bed but it wasn't there. He looked all over the basement thinking perhaps Mrs. Brown had moved it. He couldn't find it any place. Then he checked to see if the back door had been left open and found it shut and locked. He looked again to see if he could find the blanket. It just wasn't anywhere so he decided to go upstairs and ask Mrs. Brown where it was. He went up the basement stairs, had quite a time with the basement door which stuck, trotted through the kitchen and dining-room and then stood politely at the living-room door.

Mr. and Mrs. Brown were playing cribbage and arguing so they didn't see Lester for a few minutes. When Mrs. Brown happened to look up, she said, "Why Lester, have you come up to visit us?" Lester shook his head. Mrs. Brown said, "What's the matter then, is it cold down in the basement?"

Lester shook his head.

"Oh, I know," Mr. Brown said, "you want me to play ball with you, don't you, old boy?" Lester shook his head. Then, deciding that would be a very good way to get them down to the basement, he nodded his head vigorously several times. Mr. Brown beamed. "Okay, old boy," he said. "Come on down Alice and watch." Mrs. Brown said she'd like to, so they went downstairs.

But Lester, in spite of his flawless manners, went first and instead of going into the game room, stood by the furnace-room door. Mrs. Brown looked in the furnace room. "But where is your blanket?" she said. Lester shook his head. Mrs. Brown said, "Why, that's the funniest thing. I put the blue guest-room blanket on the floor here this afternoon. I wonder what could have happened to it?"

Mr. Brown, looking very embarrassed, went and got it out of the laundry chute. He said, "I didn't know it was Lester's bed, I just thought it had fallen on the floor."

Mrs. Brown spread it out on the floor and Lester carefully smoothed out the wrinkles and turned one corner over like a little pillow. Mr. and Mrs. Brown watched him in amazement.

"I've never in my life seen such a smart animal," said Mrs. Brown. "He seems almost human." Lester looked up at her quizzically. "Now you're all ready to go to bed, so I guess we'll go upstairs," said Mr. Brown.

He started toward the stairway but Lester took his hoofs and gently pushed him toward the basement door.

"Now what's the matter, old boy?" said Mr. Brown. "The basement door's locked and there's not a thing to worry about."

Mrs. Brown said, "Well of course that's the trouble. Mrs. Piggle-Wiggle told me to be sure and leave the basement door open a crack so Lester can go out in the night and get his exercise." She unlatched the door and opened it one inch.

Lester nodded approval, waited politely while they preceded him through the doorway and started up the stairs. Then he went in, lay down on the blue blanket and went to sleep.

The next morning when Christopher came downstairs and found his mother frying bacon he was shocked. He said, "My gosh, Mother, don't you have any heart at all? Last night you had spareribs for dinner and Lester almost got sick, and now this morning you are cooking bacon."

Mrs. Brown said, "Why, Chris, I thought I had a delicious dinner last night. Spareribs have always been one of your favorite foods."

Chris said, "But, Mother, spareribs are *pork*. They come from *dead pigs!*"

Mrs. Brown clapped her hand over her mouth. She said, "Oh, Chris, I didn't think about that. I'm terribly sorry. Do you suppose Lester noticed?"

Chris said, "I should say he did notice. He took one bite and then turned pale and pushed his plate away. I was going to tell you but he wouldn't let me."

Mrs. Brown said, "Come hurry, before he comes upstairs. Take this bacon in to your father. I'll give you and Lester cereal and scrambled eggs and toast for breakfast. Hurry now, take the bacon to Daddy and I'll air out the kitchen." She opened the back door and shooed the bacon smoke out with her apron so that when Lester came upstairs a few minutes later the kitchen smelled only of oatmeal and buttered toast.

As a usual thing at breakfast, Chris dumped a pitcher of cream on his mush, put on four heaping spoons of sugar, then stirred and stirred as though he were mixing cement. When the mush was exactly the right consistency and the correct degree of coolness, he would lift the bowl up to just below his chin and shovel in the mush as fast as he could swallow.

This morning, forgetting about Lester, he began his usual gluttonous proceedings, dumped the entire pitcher of cream on his mush and was just reaching for the sugar when he looked up and saw Lester looking sadly into the empty cream pitcher. Instantly he was sorry.

He said, "Oh, gee, Lester, I didn't mean to be such a pig. I mean, I mean, I mean such a glutton." Lester just looked at him. Chris said, "I'll get some more cream. Wait a minute."

Lester shook his head. He reached over and picked up

Chris' bowl of oatmeal and then carefully poured half the cream on his own cereal.

Chris said, "That's right, we'll each have half. Would you like some sugar?"

Lester nodded and helped himself carefully to two level spoons of sugar. Chris, who had watched him, did the same.

When Chris started his cement-mixer stirring, Lester reached over and took his spoon away and showed Chris how cereal should be eaten. A spoonful at a time, lifted slowly and daintily from the bowl so that each spoonful contained hot cereal, cold cream and sweet sugar.

Chris tried it. He said, "Say, Lester, this tastes much better than the old way." Lester nodded and smiled.

When Chris began to scrape his dish, Lester shook his head and pointed to his spoon, placed on the plate beside his almost empty dish.

When Chris was eating his scrambled eggs, Lester reached over and closed his mouth three times; he showed him that he must break his toast into small pieces and that he must not hold the toast in the palm of his hand when putting on jam. He made him put down his milk glass and wipe the milk mustache from his upper lip between sips. Chris obviously didn't mind these criticisms because he hugged Lester goodbye when he left for school and promised to run all the way home for lunch.

It was a beautiful morning and Mrs. Brown did a large washing. When she went to hang it on the line, Lester helped her carry the clothesbasket of wet clothes from the basement, handed her clothes pins as she needed them and then when the washing was all up he lay down on the grass in the sun, well hidden from the neighbors by two sheets and a tablecloth.

Mrs. Brown knelt down and timidly stroked his back. She said, "Thanks so much for helping with the clothes, Lester, and thank you so much for helping me with Chris's manners. I can see a great improvement already." Lester grunted a little.

By the night of Dick Thompson's dinner party, Chris's table manners were absolutely perfect and the Brown family all loved Lester so much they couldn't even think about his ever leaving. Lester came upstairs with Chris while he bathed and got dressed. He washed Christopher's back and made him wash his ears twice. He made him polish his shoes and he sent him back to his room for a clean handkerchief.

After Chris had gone Lester went out to the kitchen to wait for dinner. Noticing immediately that there was no place set for him on the kitchen table and feeling lonely for Chris and quite sad, he started down to the basement to lie on his blanket.

Mrs. Brown called to him. She said, "Lester, I thought that as long as Chris wasn't here, you would like to eat in the dining-room with Mr. Brown and me." Lester nodded his head vigorously and trotted happily after her into the dining-room.

They had roast of lamb for dinner and though Lester ate three large helpings, his table manners were so beautiful that Mr. and Mrs. Brown just stared at him in admiration.

After dinner, Mr. Brown and Lester played catch while Mrs. Brown washed the dishes. Then they all sat in the living-room and listened to the radio and waited for Christopher. He came home at ten o'clock, bursting with excitement and filled with tales of Africa and lions. Everyone listened to his stories, heard what the Thompsons had to eat and what Uncle Charlie looked like and then went to bed.

The next morning Mrs. Brown had two telephone calls. The first one made her very proud. It was from Mrs. Thompson and she said that she just had to call Mrs. Brown and tell her that in all her life she had never seen such a beautifully behaved boy as Christopher. "His table manners are simply perfect," she said and Mrs. Brown smiled and smiled.

The second telephone call was from Mrs. Piggle-Wiggle and it made Mrs. Brown very sad. Mrs. Piggle-Wiggle asked Mrs. Brown how she liked Lester and Mrs. Brown said, "Oh, Mrs. Piggle-Wiggle, he has such perfectly beautiful manners; he is such a wonderful teacher and he is so charming that I feel just like crying when I think of all the times I've said that people are pigs, or ate like pigs or were selfish like pigs."

Mrs. Piggle-Wiggle said, "Well, of course all pigs aren't like Lester but he certainly is a dear and I hate to take him away from you so soon but I have just had an emergency call from Mrs. Burbank. Tell Christopher to bring Lester over on his way back to school this noon."

When Mrs. Brown said goodbye to Lester she had tears in her eyes and she thought he seemed a little sad at leaving.

THE INTERRUPTERS

$\mathcal{W}$hat do you suppose happened at the Garden Club today?" Mrs. Franklin asked her husband at dinner. Before Mr. Franklin could answer, Benji Franklin said, "Hey, Dad, I'm the pitcher of our team."

"Please don't interrupt, Benjamin," Mr. Franklin said. "Now, what happened at your garden club, Carol?"

"Well, John, I won the first prize for my arrangement of forsythia and driftwood," Mrs. Franklin said.

"The thing I don't understand about flower arrangements . . ." Mr. Franklin began when Stevie interrupted to say, "I caught a little green frog on my way home from school."

"Don't interrupt Daddy," Mrs. Franklin said. "Now what is it you don't understand about flower arrangements, John?"

"I don't see why you don't use flowers. Why you always have to use—" Sally Franklin interrupted. She said, "I need a pair of new roller skates. My roller skates are so slow I'm ashamed to skate on them and—"

"You had roller skates last spring and I need a new baseball—" Benji began, when Stevie interrupted to say, "This little frog was just sitting there—" Benji interrupted. "I can't pitch with that old ball—" Sally said, "Everybody in our block has new roller skates and I—"

As each child interrupted the talk became louder and louder until they were all shouting.

Mr. Franklin shouted louder than anyone, "BE QUIET ALL OF YOU. I desire to finish my thought. Now, the thing I don't understand about flower arrangements is why you don't use flowers. Why you always have to stuff sticks or old weeds or seedpods or broken flower pots in with the flowers."

Mrs. Franklin smiled indulgently at her husband and began explaining, "Flower arranging is an art—" when Sally interrupted, "If I try to make figure eights with a broken strap I'll probably kill myself. Ball bearings only cost—" Stevie interrupted her, "Would you like to see my little frog? I've got—" Benji interrupted him. "Doesn't anyone in this family care whether I'm captain of my baseball team? Doesn't anyone—"

"STOP INTERRUPTING!" Mr. Franklin shouted. There was quiet for a minute. Mrs. Franklin began again.

"Flower arranging is an art—" There she was interrupted by a loud scream from Sally. "Mother, Daddy, Stevie has a frog in his pocket! I heard it. I hearrrrrrrd it—eeeeeeeeeee!"

"Stevie," said Mrs. Franklin, "do you have a frog in your pocket?"

"Well, yes, I just happen to," said Stevie, reaching in and bringing out a very small green tree frog.

"Ohhhhhhhhh," squealed Sally. "Take it away."

"Hey, lemme see it," Benji said. "Boy, he's nifty! How did you catch him?"

"It wasn't hard," Stevie said. "I was just walking along and I heard him."

"Take the frog outside," Mr. Franklin said sternly.

"Oh, Daddy, not outside," Stevie said. "He'll get away."

"Outside," Mr. Franklin repeated.

Stevie started slowly to his feet, carefully holding the frog between his cupped hands. When he got to the kitchen door he turned to his mother, "Say, Mother," he said, "this frog would be just right for your flower arrangements."

"Why, Stevie, what a wonderful idea," said Mrs. Franklin excitedly. "But how would I get him to stay in the bowl?"

"Oh, Cheeper'd stay," said Stevie. "He's awful tame. He does just anything I want him to."

"If he's so tame and does what you want him to, put him outside and tell him to WAIT THERE FOR YOU," Mr. Franklin said.

Benji said, "Oh, gee, Daddy, can't we put him in the basement. He'll get lost outside."

Mr. Franklin said, "All right, put him in the basement but put him in a box or something. Now, Carol, dear, what were you telling me about flower arranging?"

Mrs. Franklin smiled and began again, "I said flower arranging is an art—"

"Hey, Daddy, is this box all right?" Stevie called from the kitchen where he was standing on a high stool rummaging around on a shelf.

Mr. Franklin said, "Don't interrupt, your mother is talking."

Mrs. Franklin began, "Flower arranging is—" Stevie came into the dining-room, poked at his father's arm and whispered, in a loud hoarse whisper, "Is this box all right, Daddy?"

Mr. Franklin put his hands up to his head. "I'm going crazy," he said. "Interrupt! Interrupt! Interrupt! That's all these children do. We haven't finished a sentence in this house for weeks. Now Stevie, you stand right here and wait until your mother finishes explaining that flower arranging is an art," and Stevie did although it took Mrs. Franklin almost fifteen minutes. It was very uninteresting to him and his frog kept cheeping loudly.

The very second Mrs. Franklin finished her explanation of flower arranging, Stevie said, "Hey, Daddy, is this box all right?"

"Yes, yes, yes," said Mr. Franklin. "Go put the frog in it. Carol, do you suppose that Mrs. Piggle-Wiggle knows a cure for interrupting?"

"I wouldn't be surprised," said Mrs. Franklin. "I'll call—"

Sally interrupted, "If I had new roller skates, I could do a double figure—"

"What do frogs eat?" called Benji from the basement stairs.

"—eight backwards," finished Sally.

"Are flies all right?" called Stevie.

Sally said, "I could help with the dishes every night—"

"I mean dead flies?" called Stevie.

"To pay for them and it wouldn't—" Sally began.

Benji yelled, "Stevie has the box half full of ole dead flies. Won't that kill this little frog?"

Sally said, "If you don't leave roller skates outside—"

"Hey, Mom, Benji's dumpin' flies all over the basement stairs," Stevie called.

"CALL MRS. PIGGLE-WIGGLE RIGHT NOW!" roared Mr. Franklin.

So Mrs. Franklin did.

Mrs. Piggle-Wiggle said, "I have some wonderful magic interrupter powder. It comes with two little blowers and I would suggest that you and Mr. Franklin each use one. At the dinner table when you start to talk, have Mr. Franklin blow the powder at the children. When he talks, you blow the powder on the children. There will be no interrupting, I'll guarantee. Why don't you send Benji and Stevie over for it now while it's still light outside?"

Mrs. Franklin said she would, thanked Mrs. Piggle-Wiggle and hung up.

Benji and Stevie were glad to go because they loved Mrs. Piggle-Wiggle and anyway they wanted to show her their frog, Cheeper. While they were gone Mrs. Franklin and Sally washed the dishes and Mr. Franklin smoked his pipe and read the paper.

When the boys came home they gave the package to their mother and then went right to the basement to fix their frog because Mrs. Piggle-Wiggle had given them a box of

frog food and they were anxious to see if Cheeper would eat it. They asked Sally to come to the basement with them but she had a map to draw so went up to her room.

When they were alone Mr. and Mrs. Franklin opened Mrs. Piggle-Wiggle's package. It contained a little can of white powder and two little blowers. The directions on the can said, "INTERRUPTER POWDER. Place a small amount of the powder in the bowl of the blower, then when you wish to stop an interrupter, blow a little of the powder in his face. The powder cannot be seen or felt but it is wiser to blow it when the interrupter is not looking."

Mr. and Mrs. Franklin were most anxious to try the magic powder but knew that it would be wiser to wait until breakfast time the next morning, so they sent the children to bed early and spent the rest of the evening in blissful uninterrupted quiet.

Just before they went to bed they filled their little magic blowers and put them on the table in the upper hall, where they wouldn't forget them. The next morning they could hardly wait for the children to come to breakfast and begin interrupting.

When at last they had all assembled, on purpose Mr. Franklin began a long dull story about the value of getting up early. Before the children had a chance to see how long and dull the story was going to be and while they were all turned toward Mr. Franklin, Mrs. Franklin took her little blower and blew the magic powder on them.

Then Mr. Franklin began, "When I was a boy I loved to get up early. Nobody ever had any trouble getting me out of bed. I used to get up early every single morning. At first I used to get up late, about six-thirty. Then I started getting up at five-thirty, then I decided that that wasn't early enough so I began getting up at four-thirty—"

Benji started to interrupt. "There's a boy at school—" he began but that was as far as he got. His mouth opened and closed like a goldfish but no sound came out.

Mr. Franklin looked at him, smiled and continued, "at four-thirty so I could see the beauty of the sunrise and hear the early morning sounds—"

Stevie tried to interrupt. "My teacher says—" but that was as far as he got. His mouth snapped open and shut and snapped open and snapped closed like a spectacle case but no sound came out.

Sally began to laugh and to point at the boys. "Hey, look," she began, then her mouth just stayed open, wide open. She looked like a board with a knothole in it.

Mr. Franklin looked around at his gaping children, smiled with pleasure and continued, "sounds of bird song and peace; could smell the delicious fragrance of flowers drenched with dew; could watch the sun come up and give the gray earth form and color." He finished his story in complete uninterrupted silence.

Then Mrs. Franklin said, "John, do you think I should have the Weavers to dinner Friday night. They are terrible bores but we do owe—"

Benji tried to interrupt. He said, "Today is the—" But no one ever found out what today was because his mouth just stayed open like Sally's.

Mrs. Franklin continued, "owe them a dinner and the Chalmers are not too—"

Sally started to say something, "You told me not—" the

sound stopped but her mouth snapped open and snapped shut and snapped open and snapped shut like a spectacle case. There was no sound.

Stevie said, "Whatsa matter—" but the words seemed to choke in his throat and his mouth opened and shut and opened and shut like a goldfish.

Mrs. Franklin continued, "Chalmers are not too bright themselves so it would really be killing two birds with one stone."

"Which is a fine way to talk about your cooking," said Mr. Franklin, laughing. The children didn't say anything, they just sat there like a knothole, a fish and a spectacle case.

That afternoon Mrs. Franklin had some of the ladies from her garden club for tea. She asked Sally to pass the sandwiches and the boys to keep the kettle boiling and to wash the cups. Sally had on her best ruffly white pinafore and the boys washed clear above the water marks on their wrists and everything went very smoothly until Mrs. Wintersmelt began explaining the value of chicken wire in flower arrangements.

All the ladies were listening in a most eager way when suddenly the kitchen door was flung open and Benji and Stevie came racing into the living room.

"Isn't it water crest, Mother?" Stevie said.

"Aw lissen to that dummy," said Benji. "Anybody knows it is water cresk."

"Boys," said Mrs. Franklin. "Go out to the kitchen. You have INTERRUPTED Mrs. Wintersmelt." The boys went sheepishly out to the kitchen and Mrs. Franklin excused herself, picked up her little blower from the hall table and followed them. Just as they turned the corner from the pantry to the kitchen she covered them with the magic powder, then gave them a short firm lecture.

Then just for safety's sake she called to Sally, who was listening outside the door anyway, hoping the boys might be slapped a little, and told her to fix some more lemon slices. When she was getting the lemons out of the cooler and had her back turned, Mrs. Franklin sprayed her with the magic powder, then went back to the living-room to catch the end of Mrs. Wintersmelt's advice on chicken wire.

When Mrs. Wintersmelt had acknowledged the clapping that followed her talk, Mrs. Backscratcher began a talk on how much more effective flower arrangements are when you don't use flowers at all. She was well into her subject and was describing a lovely flower arrangement she had brought with her made of toothpicks and bottle caps, when Sally tried to interrupt her to tell her that they made things out of toothpicks at school. She took hold of Mrs. Backscratcher's arm and began, "We make—" but that was as far as she got. Her mouth just stayed open.

Mrs. Backscratcher stopped talking and stared at her. "Does the child stammer?" she asked Mrs. Franklin.

"No," said Mrs. Franklin in a most exasperated way, "she interrupts, which is worse. Go out to the kitchen, Sally." Sally, her mouth still open wide, went.

Mrs. Backscratcher continued, "You know, ladies, that is a very funny thing. That little girl's open mouth reminds me of a lovely arrangement I saw in Chicago made out of a knothole and a bunch of grass."

The ladies all moved their chairs closer.

Mrs. Franklin from the corner of her eye saw the kitchen

door swing open. Benji and Stevie edged into the hall and began, "Mom, Stevie—" "Mom, Benji—" that was all. They just stood there, their mouths opening and closing and no sound coming out. The ladies all stopped listening to Mrs. Backscratcher and peered out at the children.

A Mrs. Wartsnoggle, who was deaf and wore an ear phone, thought the children were saying something and so she turned her ear phone up as high as it would go, then when she still couldn't hear anything she took out the batteries and tapped on them.

Mrs. Franklin got up and pushed the boys back into the kitchen. Mrs. Backscratcher continued, "two pipe cleaners and a vanilla cork put into an empty sardine can—"

Only to Mrs. Wartsnoggle it came out "TWO PIPE CLEANERS AND A VANILLA CORK PUT INTO AN EMPTY SARDINE CAN!" until she turned her ear phone down.

For the rest of the afternoon the children stayed in the kitchen but, just to be on the safe side, Mrs. Franklin kept the little blower in her knitting bag.

At dinner, Mr. Franklin blew so much magic powder on the children that they didn't even start to interrupt. Just turned their heads toward the person they hoped to interrupt and opened and closed their mouths, or kept their mouths open or snapped open and snapped shut like a spectacle case.

Finally Sally, during a pause in the conversation and when she was not interrupting, asked her mother and daddy what made Benji and Stevie and her suddenly stop talking and look like fish, so Mr. and Mrs. Franklin ex-

plained about the Magic Interrupter powder and showed the children the little blowers.

Benji said, "I think that's a good idea but I think you and Daddy should have some too. You interrupt lots of times."

Mr. Franklin said, "Benjamin, your mother and I are grown up."

Mrs. Franklin said, "I think Benjamin is right," and she blew a big puff of powder on Mr. Franklin. He grabbed his blower and blew some on her. Then everyone laughed.

A few minutes later, Mr. Franklin tried to interrupt Mrs. Franklin's rather long-drawn-out description of her tea and he was certainly surprised to have his mouth open wide and stay open and no sound come out.

Then Mrs. Franklin tried to interrupt Benjamin's night before last's dream which turned out to be a rehash of *Treasure Island*. Her mouth opened and shut and opened and shut like a cod. My, the children and Mr. Franklin laughed.

Of course the Franklins used up all the magic powder in two weeks, but its spell lasted and to this day nobody in that family ever interrupts anyone else. It is just a pleasure to tell a story at the Franklins' house. You can always count on uninterrupted eager attention, even if you are the biggest bore in the world.

THE HEEDLESS BREAKER

It was such a beautiful spring day. It had been dark and rainy in the morning when Sharon left the house for school but now at 3:15 the sun was shining, there was a nice little springy breeze to send the clouds tumbling and the big old peach tree in the Rogers' front yard was covered with fat pink buds.

Sharon Rogers said goodbye to her best friend, Mary Lou Robertson, banged open the front gate, and left it swinging, dropped her library book in the wet grass as she knelt down to hug her little dachshund Missy, forgot about the library book, went running up to the front door, banged it open and shut, tossed her galoshes and raincoat onto the floor of the hall closet, dashed into the living-room to kiss her mother, didn't notice that her mother had

70

company and was drinking tea, grabbed her around the waist from behind in a big bear hug which sent the teacup flying across the room where it hit a little table and broke into a dozen pieces and it sprayed tea all over the rug.

Mrs. Rogers sighed as she kissed Sharon and said, "Sharon, dear, please try to be more careful. I love to have you hug me but won't you please look first to see if I have a cup of tea in my hands. Now say how-do-you-do to Mrs. Green then run and get the dishcloth."

Sharon's sweet blue eyes filled with tears and she said, "How-do-you-do, Mrs. Green. Oh, Mother, I forgot. I'm so sorry."

Her mother said, "I'm sure you are, dear. Now hurry and get the dishcloth before the tea dries and stains the rug."

Sharon ran to the kitchen and Mrs. Rogers sighed as she picked up the pieces of broken cup. This was the eleventh cup Sharon had broken this week, to say nothing of the seven plates, four vases, a blue sugar bowl and a mirror shattered the week before.

There was a splintering crash from the kitchen. Mrs. Rogers excused herself to Mrs. Green and still carrying the pieces of broken cup, hurried to the kitchen. She found Sharon sitting in the middle of the floor surrounded by broken spice jars and spilled spices. The little old spice cupboard which Mrs. Rogers had inherited from her grandmother was clinging to the wall by one nail, empty and with one of its fragile shelves splintered.

Mrs. Rogers said, "What in the world happened? I thought I sent you for the dishcloth."

Sharon said, "Well, the dishcloth was hanging on the

little rack by the spice cupboard and I was reaching for it when I remembered the hard candy you keep up there on that high shelf so I climbed up on the stove and just put one foot on the spice cupboard and I didn't know it would break. I'm sorry, Mother."

Mrs. Rogers sighed as she reached for the dishcloth still hanging on the little rack. She said, "Oh, Sharon, won't you please try to be more careful and not so heedless. Now pick up this mess and go up and change your clothes. Your cookies and milk are on the table." She took the dishcloth and went through the swinging door to the dining-room.

Sharon jumped to her feet, rushed over and grabbed the broom and began sweeping vigorously at the spilled spices, forgetting or not noticing in her heedless hurry that the largest and fullest jar of spice had been one of black pepper. Mrs. Rogers coming through the swinging door to return the dishcloth and fill the teapot, caught a large broomful of pepper square in the face. "Kachoo, kachoo, achoo!" she sneezed as the teapot lid rattled and Sharon continued to spread the pepper through the kitchen.

"Pepper! Be careful, achoo, achoo!" said Mrs. Rogers rubbing her smarting eyes. Sharon stopped sweeping. "Pepper, where?" She knelt down to look at the floor, carelessly letting go of the broom which fell down and rapped poor Mrs. Rogers across the instep.

"Ouch!" she yelled, bending down to rub her sore foot just as Sharon, who hadn't noticed that she had dropped the broom on her mother, grabbed a handful of pepper and without looking thrust it up over her shoulder and said, "Is this pepper, Mother?"

Mrs. Rogers caught this handful of pepper right in the left eye. She gave a yelp of pain, rushed to the sink and began throwing cold water in her face. Sharon instantly sorry said, "Oh, Mother, I didn't see you. I'm terribly sorry."

Mrs. Rogers said, "GO UPSTAIRS BEFORE I LOSE MY TEMPER!"

"Well, you don't have to be so cross about it," Sharon said, banging open the swinging door which caught Mrs. Green, who was just coming out to see if she could help, between the eyes and knocked off her rimless spectacles.

"My heavens, what happened?" said Mrs. Green, who couldn't see without her spectacles.

"Oh, I'm so sorry," said Sharon. "Did I hurt you?" She stepped forward solicitously and there was a loud crunch. "Oh," said Sharon, "look, I've stepped on something."

Mrs. Green said, "Oh, no! My glasses?" and Sharon said, "Oh, yes," and began to cry.

Mrs. Rogers, who was still at the sink trying to wash the pepper out of her eyes, called, "Sharod Rogers, kachoo! Go, kachoo! kachoo! right, kachoo, up kachoo, stairs, kachoo, and stay id your roob, kachoo!"

Sharon went.

Poor Mrs. Green knelt down and began fumbling around on the floor for the broken glasses. She was hoping that there might be one glass or perhaps a fairly good-sized piece of one glass that she could hold up to her eye and see to go home. She found the glasses at last, but they had been ground to dust by Sharon's heel. So Mrs. Rogers, her eyes red and swollen, and sneezing every five seconds, had to lead her friend home. Sharon from her bedroom window watched them grope their way along the street through the spring afternoon and it made her cry harder than ever because they looked like two feeble old ladies who had just been to a funeral.

At half-past-six Mr. Rogers opened Sharon's door slowly and carefully, then guarding himself with his arm he said, "Dinner is ready. You may give me one kiss, Careless Carrie, but be gentle and try not to black my eye or break my arm."

Sharon gave her daddy a hug and said, "Oh, Daddy, I don't mean to be so careless. I didn't mean to break Mrs. Green's glasses."

He said, "I know you didn't, Chickabiddy, but that doesn't help Mrs. Green see. You must learn to move more slowly. To look before you leap. You're only eight years old and I'd like to keep you for another twelve or thirteen years at least but at the rate you're breaking things I won't be able to afford it. Let's see, last week you broke eleven cups, there are fifty-two weeks in a year and 52×11 is 572 cups a year and we have at least twelve more years to go—that would be six thousand, eight hundred and sixty-four cups. Wow!"

They went down to dinner and Sharon was very careful and didn't jerk her chair or bang the table as she sat down. When she cleared off the table she moved slowly and carefully and only spilled a little French dressing in her mother's lap. She continued to be very careful while she was helping with the dishes and as a result didn't chip or break a single thing.

When the last dish was dried and the dishtowels were

hung up, her mother gave her a kiss and said that she was
awfully sorry about the mishaps of the afternoon and now
to give her father a kiss and hurry to bed. Sharon was so
happy that she had not been heedless that she rushed into
the den to tell her father, forgot that the door stuck, gave it
a hard jerk, slipped on the rug, fell against the hall table
and knocked over and broke the little red chinese bowl of
white hyacinths. Mrs. Rogers cried because the red bowl
had been a wedding present, Mr. Rogers shouted because
the carpenter who was supposed to have fixed the door
charged so much and didn't do anything and Sharon cried
because her heedlessness had spoiled the whole evening for
her mother and father.

After Sharon had gone to bed, Mr. and Mrs. Rogers sat
up very late worrying about Sharon's heedlessness. Mrs.
Rogers thought perhaps Sharon should have dancing lessons to make her more graceful. Mr. Rogers thought she
should have a sound spanking every time she broke anything. Mrs. Rogers thought that elocution lessons were
what Sharon needed to give her poise. Mr. Rogers thought
Sharon should pay for everything she broke out of her
25¢ a week allowance. Mrs. Rogers wondered if Sharon's
eyes needed testing. Mr. Rogers said that he thought that a
good sound spanking *and* paying for everything she broke
was the solution. Mrs. Rogers said that she had heard that
trouble with the inner ear affected children's balance, perhaps this was a result of the chicken pox. Mr. Rogers said
that as Sharon had had the chicken pox four years ago and
had only been a heedless breaker for two weeks, he thought
that theory was ridiculous. He thought that a good sound
spanking, paying for everything broken and not going to

the moving picture show on Saturday afternoon was the answer. Now when he was a boy, when he broke the little buck saw with which he had to saw great heaps of wood every single day after school rain or snow, his father had made him pay for it all himself and he had to earn the money after he had sawed the wood. Mrs. Rogers said that she thought she would go to bed and read. Mr. Rogers said that that was the trouble with Sharon, Mrs. Rogers refused to face facts.

The next morning Sharon wakened to find sunbeams in her eyes and a fat robin sitting in the tree outside her window and scolding her. Sharon said, "Oh, you darling robin, I'll get right up." She jumped out of bed and started for the window, forgetting that the night before she had been oiling her roller skates and had left them in a heap on the floor right in the middle of the room. The poor little robin was surprised and very scared when Sharon tripped over the roller skates and came banging against the window screen so hard she bulged it way out. The robin flew away and Sharon began to cry, which was a very poor way to start a lovely spring day.

Then Sharon jumped into the shower without her shower cap and got her thick brown hair soaking; then, when she was finally dressed and ready for breakfast, she just happened to find her favorite old golf ball and gave it one bounce on the stairs and it got away, bounced way up high and broke off three of the crystal danglers on the hall chandelier; then she sat down for breakfast, forgetting about the table leg (in spite of having been told about it every single morning for the last three years), and when her knees hit the table leg it joggled the table and slopped the orange juice, the coffee and the cream. Mr. and Mrs. Rogers just looked at each other. Sharon, very red in the face, began eating her cereal.

When she finally left for school, after shaking fountain-pen ink all over the hall carpet and turning the house upside down looking for the library book which was finally found all wrinkled and wet down by the gate, Mr. Rogers said, "I still think a spanking, paying for everything she breaks, and not going to the movies on Saturday is the answer."

Mrs. Rogers said, "If you tell me about that old buck saw which your nasty, stingy father made you pay for once again I'll scream."

Mr. Rogers said stiffly, "I had no intention of telling you about the buck saw. I was going to ask you if you had thought of calling Mrs. Piggle-Wiggle to see if she has any suggestions for curing our Little Heedless Breaker."

Mrs. Rogers said, "Oh, Herbie, darling, of course. Mrs. Piggle-Wiggle. Why didn't I think of it? She'll be sure to know of something. Oh, you're so smart, dear!" She gave Mr. Rogers a kiss and he went beaming off to work.

When Mrs. Piggle-Wiggle heard about Sharon's heedlessness she said, "Oh I have just the thing for that. It's a magic powder which you sprinkle in a Heedless Breaker's bed. The magic powder is absorbed during the night and the next morning when Miss Heedless Breaker gets out of bed she will find that she can only move very, very, very slowly. I'll send you enough for two days which should do the trick. Let's see, this is Thursday, I'll send the powder over tomorrow afternoon. Goodbye, Mrs. Rogers, and don't worry." Mrs. Piggle-Wiggle hung up.

Mrs. Rogers called Mr. Rogers right away to tell him what Mrs. Piggle-Wiggle had said. Mr. Rogers said, "Sounds fine, but if that doesn't work I still think my methods should be tried. A good sound spanking would at least make Sharon careful about sitting down." He laughed callously.

Mrs. Rogers said, "Ummm, ummmm. Don't be late tonight, dear, we're having cheese soufflé."

That afternoon, in spite of great precautions on Mrs. Rogers' part, Sharon tipped over her milk, stepped on Missy's foot, broke a basement window, and stepped hard on two poor struggling shoots of Mrs. Rogers' most prized delphinium. With each little accident, Sharon seemed truly repentant and promised tearfully to be more careful, but in five or ten minutes crash, bang and something else would be broken.

Just before dinner she whizzed up to the back steps to take off her roller skates, of course didn't look behind her and sat down splash in Missy's water dish. Mary Lou Robertson laughed until tears ran down her cheeks but Sharon was mad. She ripped off her skates, threw them on the porch and stamped upstairs to her room.

When Mr. Rogers came home early because of the cheese soufflé and found that it wasn't quite ready, he decided to do a little pruning. So, grabbing the pruning shears and with his cutting eye aimed toward anything in the garden showing signs of life, he threw open the back door, strode out into the spring evening, tripped over Sharon's roller skates, took a flying leap off the porch, landed with one foot in the garbage can and the other on the rake which Sharon had left lying by the steps after retrieving her ball

from the porch roof. As he stepped on the tines of the rake the handle came up and hit him smartly in the nose.

Mr. Rogers was so mad he roared. "Marjorie! Sharon! MARJORIESHARON!" When Sharon timidly opened the back door he pointed at the roller skates and said, "DID YOU LEAVE THOSE SKATES THERE? DID YOU LEAVE THIS RAKE HERE?"

"Yes," said Sharon in a tiny little squeak of a voice.

"Well," said her daddy, "your careless heedlessness has almost lost me my life. I am now going to give you a spanking." And he did and so dinner was a snuffling red-eyed meal filled with cold looks and long silences and the cheese soufflé which was delicious.

Mrs. Rogers was secretly pleased to note that Friday, in spite of Mr. Rogers' spanking, Sharon seemed more heedless than ever. She dropped the waffle iron and tipped over the syrup at breakfast; she banged through the swinging door into her mother who was carrying a platter of sausages so that sausages flew through the air like little zeppelins and a big blob of grease landed on Sharon's bangs; she turned on the water in the kitchen sink so hard it sprayed all over her clean middy blouse and soaked the front of her nice clean pleated skirt; she banged the front door so hard the house shook and Mrs. Rogers' new philodendron fell off the window sill and the pot broke into a million pieces and dirt scattered all over the hall.

The last the Rogers saw of their daughter she zoomed through the front gate on one roller skate, banged into Mary Lou, who was waiting for her, so that Mary Lou went flouncing off to school alone, took off the roller skate, tossed it over the fence into a bed of crocuses and ran after her best friend. Mr. and Mrs. Rogers watched her until she rounded the corner then they went back to the breakfast table and had another cup of coffee.

Mr. Rogers said, "If Mrs. Piggle-Wiggle's magic powder doesn't work, I think we should move into an old bomb shelter until Sharon grows out of this awful Heedless Breaker stage."

Mrs. Rogers said, "I still think that dancing lessons might be the answer."

Mr. Rogers laughed. He said, "Yeah, I can just see her leaping around kicking the teacher in the eye and knocking down the other pupils. The only difference would be that she'd be busting things to music." They both laughed.

About four-thirty that afternoon, Larry Gray brought Mrs. Rogers a package from Mrs. Piggle-Wiggle. Inside the package was a small can, like a talcum powder can, with holes in the top. The can was marked "CURE FOR HEEDLESS BREAKERITIS" and the directions read: "Sprinkle powder thoroughly over Heedless Breaker's bed. Use two nights in succession."

Mrs. Rogers, who had been waiting for the powder before making Sharon's bed, ran upstairs, threw back the covers and dusted the entire bottom sheet with the powder. There wasn't much left when she got through but she thought, "The first day is the most important anyway."

That night Sharon went to bed, having no idea what was in store for her, and slept soundly, but both Mr. and Mrs. Rogers were restless and nervous and dreamed terrible dreams about magic and their poor little girl.

When Sharon woke up the next morning, she was very surprised to find both her mother and father standing by her bed staring at her. "How do you feel?" they asked anxiously. "Sleepy," said Sharon and yawned, very slowly.

"Hurry and get dressed," said her mother. "I'm going to make French toast."

"Goody," said Sharon and started to leap out of bed. Instead of leaping, she was very surprised to find herself moving like a queen, slowly and regally. Her body felt very, very heavy but smooth and sort of floaty. It was very pleasant.

Sharon's usual custom in the morning was to jerk out her bureau drawers so hard, they almost always came all the way out and dumped everything on the floor. This morning she went over to her bureau to get some clean socks, reached for the drawer handles and was surprised to see how slowly and carefully her fingers grasped them. She tried to jerk the drawers out but her arms moved back slowly and the drawer pulled out gently and just far enough for her to be able to reach her socks without any trouble. When she had finished she tried to give the drawer a shove, but her hand wouldn't come away. It pushed the drawer all the way in, carefully and slowly.

When Sharon sat down in her little rocking chair to put on her socks, she found that she moved slowly and as though controlled by strings, like a puppet.

Usually Sharon jammed her feet into her socks so hard that often her toes would go poking right through the end. This morning her foot wouldn't poke. It moved forward slowly and gracefully and Sharon found herself pulling on her socks with as much care as her mother put on her nylon stockings. Her socks looked nice too, the tops were turned down and even and the heels were on her heels, not in front as they often were.

It actually didn't take Sharon any longer to dress this new careful way, because she didn't have to stop and get other socks after poking holes in the first ones and she didn't have to stop and cry and rub her knees, her toes or elbows after tripping over, bumping into or knocking down the furniture.

She saw her old golf ball on her desk and carried it down to breakfast but she didn't bounce it on the stairs because she was moving slowly and had time to remember what had happened before, how it had bounced and broken her mother's crystal chandelier. When she walked slowly into breakfast, carefully pulled out her chair, sat down gracefully without bumping the table leg, and daintily unfolded her napkin, her mother and father looked at each other and beamed. Breakfast was a gracious, quiet, pleasant meal and the French toast was delicious.

After breakfast Sharon washed the dishes for her mother and her new slow careful way of doing things made it seem like an easy job. She was through in no time with nothing broken and everything put away in the right place. Her mother was so surprised and pleased when she opened the ice-box door to find that Sharon had not, as was her usual practice, put in big plates with tiny dabs of food on them, had not balanced the syrup jug on a glass of milk, had not crowded things so that when Mrs. Rogers opened the door at least three dishes jumped out at her and crashed.

Sharon was sweeping the back porch and Mrs. Rogers peeked out the door and watched her in amazement. Instead of standing in the middle of the porch and sweeping from side to side with big careless sweeps so that dog bones, dust, crumbs and leaves went flying in every direction including her hair, Sharon was sweeping with small careful strokes, and everything was in a neat little pile. Her mother tapped on the door and waved at her. Sharon slowly raised her head and smiled.

After a while when Mary Lou, Molly O'Toole and Susan Gray came over to roller skate, Mrs. Rogers was terribly pleased to see that Sharon was the most graceful skater of all. Mrs. Rogers used to be afraid to watch Sharon skate because she skated like double-greased lightning and banged into trees, tripped over stones and fell flat on her face and used to do very dangerous heedless things like skating down a hill backwards. Now she sailed down the street on one foot, as airy and graceful as a leaf. She even won when they had a race because her strokes were long and she watched where she was going and avoided rough places.

When she came in for lunch, Mrs. Rogers almost fainted to see her carefully unlatch and open the gate, then close it after her. She was carrying her roller skates and she put them in the hall closet where they belonged, instead of tossing them on the porch.

At lunch, instead of gulping a mouthful of hot soup, giving a yell and spraying it around the kitchen, Sharon waited a little for the soup to cool, then ate it slowly and daintily. When she had finished she said to her mother, "You know, Mother, I feel so funny today. Sort of slow and floaty and everything seems so easy. I don't bump into things, I haven't broken a single thing, and I can roller skate just beautifully."

Mrs. Rogers said, "I've noticed it, Sharon. You move slowly and gracefully like a queen. It must be that you had a very restful sleep last night."

Sharon said, "I think that must be it." She kissed her mother and went upstairs to change her clothes.

Instead of whamming through the swinging door so that it clanged against the wall on the other side, clumping up the stairs and crashing open the door of her room, Sharon slipped through the swinging door, went up the stairs on tiptoes and gently clicked open the door of her room. Mrs. Rogers had tears of joy in her eyes as she got out all her nice little knick-knacks and put them back on the shelves and tables. She even called Mrs. Green, explained the wonderful change in Sharon and invited her over for tea.

Mrs. Green came but she approached the Rogers' house warily and with great caution as though it were a bomb.

Sharon was just leaving for the moving-picture show but she stopped and greeted Mrs. Green, apologized again for breaking her glasses, and was so quiet, gentle and charming that Mrs. Green couldn't believe it was Sharon and thought that probably it was really a secret twin sister.

When Mrs. Rogers explained about Mrs. Piggle-Wiggle's magic powder, Mrs. Green was terribly interested and asked if she could borrow a little to use on her husband when he played golf. "If he misses a shot," she told Mrs. Rogers, "he roars like a lion and breaks the clubs over his knee. He's broken two sets already and it is only April."

Mrs. Rogers ran upstairs to get the magic powder because she knew she wouldn't need it any more.

THE NEVER-WANT-TO-GO-TO-SCHOOLER

"Seven-thirty, time to get up," called Mrs. Jones
loudly and cheerfully from the foot of the stairs. Julie
and Linda jumped out of bed and began to race getting
dressed. From Jody and Jan's room there was the sound
of one person getting up and loud groans.

"I feel terrible," groaned Jody from the upper bunk.

"Aw," said Jan, "you just don't want to go to school.
You did the same thing last week. Groaned and moaned
and felt sick until the rest of us left for school and then you
felt fine."

"Oh, is that so? And how do you know so much, Dr.
Jones?" said Jody, leaning out of the upper bunk and forgetting to groan.

"I know," said Jan as he tied his shoes, "because somebody was using my toolbox while I was at school. Some-

body who nicked the chisel and left the hammer out on the sidewalk by the maple tree."

Jody said, "I was fixing the treehouse and I did not nick your old chisel. Dick Thompson nicked it and you know he did."

Jan said, "Dick nicked it just a little, now it has a bigger nick in it, I measured."

Jody said, "When I'm ten and get my own toolbox I won't let you even walk past it. I'll never ever even let you see inside it."

There was the sound of brisk footsteps on the stairs. Jody threw himself back in bed and began to groan. Mrs. Jones appeared at the doorway. She said, "I have made waffles for breakfast this morning. Hurry, boys."

Jan said, "I'm all ready as soon as I wash my face and hands. Ole-pretend-he's-sick-Jody is groanin' up in the upper bunk so he won't have to go to school."

Mrs. Jones walked over to the bunk, reached up and felt Jody's forehead. She said, "You haven't a speck of temperature, Jody, so stop playing possum and get up."

Jody groaned loudly and agonizingly. He said, "My stummick hurts awful. It feels like I swallowed ten knives."

Mrs. Jones looked worried. She said, "Where does it hurt, dear?"

Jody said, "Oh, all over. All over my stummick!"

Jan called from the bathroom where he was splashing a tiny little bit of water on his face. "Don't believe him, Mom, he was all right a minute ago."

Mrs. Jones said, "Jody Jones, get out of that bunk this instant! If you are sick I want a good look at you."

Jody started to sit up then crumpled in apparent agony. "Oh, oh, oh," he moaned. "My stummick is killing me."

Mrs. Jones climbed part way up the little ladder that led to the upper bunk and peered anxiously at her eight-year-old son. His eyes were closed and in the reflected light from the pine ceiling he appeared pale. Mrs. Jones patted him on the shoulder and said, "Just lie there quietly, Jody, until I get the other children off to school, then I'll bring you some tea."

Then she went downstairs and told Mr. Jones she thought they should call the doctor. Mr. Jones said, "Perhaps you had," but Jan said, "Oh, Mom, don't be dumb. There's nothing wrong with Jody at all. Just a minute ago he was leanin' over the bunk talking to me about my tools. He stayed home yesterday and the day before and he's getting so ignorant I don't even like to play with him any more."

Twelve-year-old Julie said, "Miss Robinson asked me about Jody yesterday and I told her that we thought he had amœbic dysentery."

"Amœbic dysentery!" said Mrs. Jones. "Where in the world did you get an idea like that?"

"We're studying about amœbic dysentery in hygiene," said Julie, "and personally I think Jody has all the symptoms."

"Personally, I think Jody has hydrophobia kleptomania," said Mr. Jones.

"Really?" said Julie. "What are the symptoms?"

"Pain in all cartilege and a slight stiffening of the esophagus," said Mr. Jones, solemnly buttering his waffle.

"Is Jody going to die?" wailed Linda, who was only five and didn't know what they were talking about.

"Of course not," said Mrs. Jones. "Now hurry with breakfast or you'll be late to school."

After the children had left for school and Mr. Jones had gone to the office, Mrs. Jones carried a tray up to Jody. On it were a pot of tea, two poached eggs and three pieces of toast. Between groans Jody ate every crumb.

At exactly 9:02 he came pattering down to the kitchen in his pajamas and announced that he felt a tiny bit better and thought he'd go outside for a breath of fresh air. Mrs. Jones looked at him suspiciously but he widened his large blue eyes and—as he was only eight years old, a little small for his age and seemed even smaller in ten-year-old Jan's pajamas, which he had swiped the night before because he had forgotten that he had stuffed his own in the window seat when he was cleaning up his half of the room—Mrs. Jones convinced herself that he wasn't fooling and let him go out to play.

After he had dressed, Jody helped himself to as many of Jan's tools as he could carry and went out to work on the treehouse. My, it was beautiful up there in the old maple tree! The sun made little speckles on the floor of the tree-house and two fat gray squirrels ran up and down the branches and chattered at him when he hammered.

"This is the life," said Jody happily to himself. "I'm never going to school. I'm going to be a carpenter and that's certainly something ole Miss Robinson doesn't know anything about."

"Cuttacuttacuttak," said one of the gray squirrels.

Just before the other children were due home for lunch, Jody climbed down out of the tree, went in the house and told his mother he had a little headache and felt weak. She told him to lie down on the couch with the afghan over him.

Even Julie and Jan, who came rushing in to sneer at him, thought he looked quite frail and left the room on tiptoe. Linda kissed him stickily and told him that he could take a nap with her after lunch, which made him feel slightly ashamed.

Jody had only intended to stay on the davenport until after Julie and Jan left for school, but it was so quiet in the living-room, and so comfortable on the davenport, that he fell asleep and didn't wake up until two o'clock. Twice while he was sleeping Mrs. Jones tiptoed in and felt his head. As it was cool and moist, she decided that Jody had just had a little stomach upset and it wasn't necessary to call the doctor.

As soon as he waked up, Jody got up and worked on the treehouse until ten minutes past three. Then he skinned down out of the tree, rushed in and put away Jan's tools and was again lying wistfully on the couch when Julie and Jan came home.

Jan said that he was going to work on the treehouse and did Jody want to help him. Jody said, "I'll just climb up and watch for a while. Thanks anyway, Jan." Jan watched suspiciously as Jody shinnied up the tree faster than a squirrel but he didn't say anything until he had climbed up into the treehouse himself and had seen how much work Jody had done.

"I just wish Mother could climb up here and see how

sick you are," he said, carefully examining his tools for scratches and nicks.

Jody said, "I did feel sick this morning but I got better after lunch. Hey, do you think this roof's going to be high enough?"

Jan said, "Let's make it high enough so we can have a window. Wouldn't it be fun to look out our window at the ole girls playin' in the street below?" Jody's sickness was forgotten.

Having had no lunch, Jody was starving for dinner and had two helpings of everything. When Mr. Jones passed him his second plate-full he said, "Your hydrophobia kleptomania seems to have cleared up. You'll certainly be well enough to go to school tomorrow, eh, Jody?"

Jody, making his eyes as big as he could over a mouthful of baked potato, said, "I certainly hope so, Daddy. I hate to miss school." Jan choked on his milk and Julie said that she thought all boys were disgusting and should eat out of troughs.

Mr. Jones said, "From now on, conversation at this table is to be limited to current events," and so the children had nothing to say until dinner was over.

After dinner, Linda went to bed and the other children were sent to their rooms to study. Jan went right to work on a theme he was writing entitled, "My Most Interesting Experience," but Jody got out an old magic-dot book and began filling in the pictures.

"How do you spell dangerous?" asked Jan.

"I dunno," said Jody.

There was silence for a while.

"How do you spell Africa?" asked Jan.

"I dunno," said Jody.

Silence.

"How do you spell leopard?" asked Jan.

"I dunno," said Jody.

"Gosh, don't you know anything?" said Jan.

"Sure," said Jody. "Lots of things but not spelling and I don't notice you're so good at it either. How do you spell dangerous, how do you spell Africa, how do you spell leopard?" He mimicked Jan.

Jan said, "It's just that I happen to be writing a theme and I don't have time to stop and think how to spell every single word."

"What are you writing a theme about?" asked Jody.

"My most interesting experience," said Jan.

"*Your* most interesting experience," jeered Jody. "Ha, ha, ha! What do you know about Africa and leopards?"

Jan looked embarrassed. He said, "Well, I'm pretending that one of Dick Thompson's Uncle Charlie's experiences was mine. Miss Hatfield's never been to Africa. She won't know the difference. Anyway it'll be a lot more interesting than 'The Time My Dolly Broke Her Front Tooth' or 'The Time I Found My First Crocus,' like the ole girls write."

Jody was busy filling in the last dots. He said, "Hey, look at this. It's an elephant and I thought all the time it was going to be a football field." They both laughed loudly just as Mr. Jones called that it was bedtime.

The next morning when Mrs. Jones called, "Breakfast, boys!" Jody began to groan. "Oh, oh, oh," he groaned.

"My stummick!"

Jan said, "Oh, oh, oh, my stummick, I mean I hate to go to school."

Jody ignored him. "My stummick hurts awful!" he moaned.

Jan said, "You stay out of school all the time and you won't pass. You'll be just like that old Lemmy Carson that's fourteen and in the third grade."

Jody closed his eyes and yelled louder than ever, "Oh, oh, oh, my stummick!"

Mrs. Jones came in and felt his forehead. It seemed a little hot, which could have been from the fact that Jody had his underwear on under Jan's pajamas and it could have been from his groaning.

Mrs. Jones said, "Just exactly where does it hurt, Jody?"

Jody said, "It's a sort of all-over, terrible stummick ache."

Mrs. Jones said, "You're sure you aren't just fooling, Jody?"

Jody said, "Oh, Mom, don't be silly. My stummick's killing me."

Jan said, "Don't bother with old Lemmy Carson, Mom. He's not going to school any more."

Mrs. Jones said, "Who's Lemmy Carson?"

Jan said, "Oh, he's a kid in school who is fourteen and only in the third grade."

Mrs. Jones said, "Is there anything wrong with him?"

Jan said, "Nothing except he never goes to school."

Jody said, "Oh, oh, oh, my poor stummick! It aches awful."

Mrs. Jones and Jan went downstairs. On the way down

Mrs. Jones said, "Jan, do you really think that Jody is just pretending?"

"I know he is," said Jan. "He says he's going to be a carpenter and he doesn't have to go to school."

Mrs. Jones said, "We'll just see about that," and went in to breakfast.

She didn't carry Jody any tray and so at 9:01 he came down to the kitchen and said, "Mom, dear, I feel a little better but I thought I should maybe have some er, uh," his eyes strayed toward and became glued to a large bowl of ripe bananas, "some bananas and cream and toast," he finished.

Mrs. Jones said, "Not with that stomach ache. A little tea, perhaps, but nothing else. Now march right upstairs and get back into bed." Jody went slowly and meekly.

At 9:30 he asked his mother if he could get up. She said no, loudly and firmly. At 10:00 he asked again for food. "No," said Mrs. Jones. At 10:30 he asked to get up. "No!" said his mother.

Unfortunately at 11:00 Mrs. Jones sat down to have a cup of coffee and happened to glance at the morning paper. On the front page was a heart-rending story with vivid pictures of some little starving Greek children. Mrs. Jones read the entire story twice then called to Jody to come down and get his breakfast.

He came down to the kitchen all dressed in his play clothes, in about seven seconds. Mrs. Jones gave him two shredded-wheat biscuits with sliced bananas and plenty of rich cream, two scrambled eggs, three pieces of bacon and a cinnamon bun. Jody ate it all then went out to work on the treehouse.

When the other children came home for lunch, Julie told her mother that Miss Robinson had told her that Jody was getting very far behind in his work and that if he was going to be sick long, Mrs. Jones had better go up to school and get his assignments or else arrange to have the teacher who traveled around and taught invalids come to the house.

Jan said, "Honestly, Mom, I don't see how you can be so dumb about Jody. He's just pretendin'. His ole stummick never gets sore except on school mornings."

Mrs. Jones said, "Now don't worry, children, I'll handle Jody. Julie, tell Miss Robinson I'll call her tomorrow morning."

After she had put Linda down for her nap and had washed the lunch dishes, Mrs. Jones called up her friend Mrs. Armadillo. She said, "Mrs. Armadillo, have you ever had any trouble getting Armand to go to school? I mean, does Armand like to go to school?"

"Oh, my yes," said Mrs. Armadillo. "You know Armand is only eight years old and he is in the high seventh. The teacher told me only yesterday, that actually Armand could do high-school work but I don't like to force him."

"Oh, no?" said Mrs. Jones to herself. "You started teaching him to read when he was about four months old and you started him in a private school when he was three." Aloud she said, "Well, I'm not so fortunate. You see Jody has decided that he doesn't want to go to school. Every morning he has terrible stomach aches and pains and actually seems to be suffering until after nine when he knows the bell has rung. I just can't understand it."

Mrs. Armadillo said, "Perhaps he is having trouble in school. Perhaps he isn't happy with his teacher."

Mrs. Jones said, "Oh, I'm sure he likes Miss Robinson. All the children have had her and they have all loved her."

Mrs. Armadillo said, "Well, you know some children are high strung and sensitive and the confusion of a large public school is too much for their little nervous systems. That's why we took Armand out of public school and put him in Miss Walkinshaw's School for Exceptional Children. I'll call Miss Walkinshaw right now if you wish."

Mrs. Jones said, "Oh, no, please don't bother, Mrs. Armadillo. I'll talk to Jody and see if something is troubling him. If I should decide to take him out of public school I'll let you know." She hung up. "That little earwig of an Armand," she said angrily to herself. "Imagine that, high seventh and he was only eight last month."

She called to Jody, who quickly shinnied down the tree trunk and came loping into the kitchen, beaming and expecting more food. Mrs. Jones took him on her lap. She said, "Jody, dear, is something at school bothering you?"

Jody said, "Uhh, uhh. Say, do we have any of those big ginger cookies? That kind Mrs. Maxwell bakes?"

Mrs. Jones said, "Jody, I want to talk to you about school. Do you like Miss Robinson?"

"Sure," said Jody. "She's all right. Mrs. Maxwell bakes those big ginger cookies every single Saturday."

Mrs. Jones pushed Jody rather rudely from her lap. She said, "Oh, go out and play."

Jody looking puzzled went out but called from the front gate, "I'll go down and ask Mrs. Maxwell how to make those ginger cookies if you want me to."

Mrs. Jones said, "Don't bother!" and shut the door firmly.

Then she called her friend Mrs. Wheeling and asked her if she ever had any trouble making Kitty go to school. Mrs. Wheeling said no but she knew plenty of mothers who had had trouble with Not-Want-To-Go-To-Schoolers. She told Mrs. Jones to call Mrs. Piggle-Wiggle, and Mrs. Jones did.

Mrs. Piggle-Wiggle said, "Oh, so that's where Jody's been. I wondered why I hadn't seen him pass the house lately. Well, what he needs is some Ignorance Tonic. I'll send a bottle over with Jan. Give Jody a tablespoonful right away, another after dinner, another in the morning, before lunch and before dinner tomorrow. Keep it up until he asks to go back to school." Mrs. Jones thanked Mrs. Piggle-Wiggle and hung up.

At 3:15 Jan handed his mother a package from Mrs. Piggle-Wiggle. It contained a large black bottle marked "IGNORANCE TONIC." Mrs. Jones measured a tablespoonful into a small glass, called Jody in and handed it to him.

"What's this?" Jody asked.

"Something for your pains," said his mother.

Jody said, "But they're gone now."

His mother said, "This is to prevent their returning tomorrow morning. Now drink it."

Jody did. He said, "Ummmm, tasted just like chocolate syrup."

He went out to play. He climbed up into the treehouse, sat down and began pounding in a nail upside down and with the pliers instead of the hammer.

Jan said, "Hey, what are you doing?"

Jody said, "Pounding" only he really said "Poudig" because his throat had suddenly become thick and choky.

Jan said, "Why don't you use the hammer?"

Jody said, "What's a habber?"

Jan said, "Don't try to be so funny. Here!" and handed him the hammer.

Jody took it but began pounding with the handle.

Jan grabbed the hammer away from him. "What's the matter with you, anyway?" he said.

"Duthig," Jody said and laughed a high silly giggle.

Just then Julie called from below, "Hey, boys, come on down and play Kick the Can. There's Molly and Larry and Susan and Kitty and Anne and Joan and Dick and Hubert and Patsy and Mary Lou and everybody."

So Jan and Jody climbed out of the tree and Julie began to count them out, "Ibbity, bibbity, sibbity sab. Ibbity, bibbity, casaba." Jody was it.

They told him to count to five hundred by fives. He leaned against the maple tree and closed his eyes but he couldn't think.

"Five," he said. "Let's see what comes next." He couldn't remember. He decided to count to one hundred by ones. He began in the funny thick voice he now had, "Ode, two, three," but that was as far as he could go. He couldn't remember what came after three. From all around, from one end of the block to the other he could hear the shouts of "Ready!" and he hadn't finished counting.

He decided to just stand by the tree for a while and pretend he had counted, the way Linda did. The tree trunk felt smooth and smelled spicy and delicious. He could hear the gray squirrels scolding the children from way up in the top branches. My, it was pleasant and dark behind his closed eyes. Jody fell asleep.

After about ten minutes of shouting "Ready" some of the children began stealing toward base. "Clank," Larry Gray kicked the can clear down to the corner then ran like mad. Jody did not move.

Julie come out from behind the hedge and yelled right in Jody's ear, "READY!" Jody jumped and rubbed his eyes. "Where abbi?" he said yawning.

"My gosh, Jody!" said Julie, stamping her foot. "You're too slow. You've spoiled the whole game. Now go and get the can, it's way down by the Thompsons'."

Jody ambled slowly down toward the Thompsons' but when he got down there he couldn't remember why he was there. He said good-afternoon to Mrs. Thompson, who was weeding her perennial bed, then just stood blinking in the afternoon sun. Up the street the children were all yelling. He wondered what they wanted. Mrs. Thompson said, "There's the can right there on the parking strip, Jody. Hurry and maybe you can catch them all." Jody picked up the can and ambled back toward the maple tree. As soon as he got near it the children all ran and hid. Jody put down the can and automatically began, "Ready or dot . . ." but then he couldn't remember the rest. "Ready or dot . . . Ready or dot—Ready or dot!" he said over and over again.

Julie came out from the hedge and pushed him rudely away from the tree. "Oh go and hide, dummy," she said, "I'll be it." She covered her eyes and began "Five, ten, fifteen, twenty . . ."

Jody sat down by the hedge and stared vacantly up at the sky. After a long time he noticed that there was no one around. That everyone had apparently gone home, so he went into the house. The family were at dinner.

His mother said, "Where in the world have you been? The other children came in a half an hour ago. Now go upstairs and wash and hurry." Jody went upstairs but couldn't remember what he had come up for so he went down again and in to dinner.

He sat down next to Jan, picked up a spoon and began eating. Jan said, "What are you eating with a spoon for, Baby?" Jody said, "What's a spood?" Jan and Julie laughed.

Mr. Jones said, "How do you feel tonight, Jody. Pains all gone?"

Jody repeated after him, "Paids all gode."

Mr. Jones said, "You sound as if you had a cold."

Jody said, "I'b warb edough."

Julie said, "Daddy asked you if you had a cold, dope."

Jody said, "I'b dot cold."

Jan said, "Gosh, what a dummy."

Mr. and Mrs. Jones looked at each other meaningly.

After dessert Mr. Jones said, "Let's all play 'What Johnny Has in His Pocket.' I'll start. Johnny has a ball of string in his pocket."

Linda, who was next, said, "Johnny has a ball of string and a worm in his pocket."

Julie said, "Johnny has a ball of string, a worm and an apple in his pocket."

Mrs. Jones said, "Johnny has a ball of string, a worm, an apple and a knife in his pocket."

Jan said, "Johnny has a ball of string, a worm, an apple, a knife and a nail in his pocket."

Jody said, "Joddy has a . . . Joddy has a . . ."

"Ball of string," prompted Linda.

Jody began again. "Joddy has a ball of strig, a . . . a . . ."

"And a worm," said Linda.

"Joddy has a worb," said Jody and looked around proudly.

Jan said, "Oh, let's leave the old dummy out. Come on, Daddy."

Mr. Jones said, "Come on, Jody. Johnny has a ball of string, a worm, an apple, a knife and a nail in his pocket."

Jody said, "I cadt rebeber all that. I dodt wadt to play."

He began to cry and Mrs. Jones sent him to bed.

The next morning Jody didn't have to pretend he was sick because when he waked up the other children had already gone to school. Jody got dressed and went downstairs but he couldn't find his mother. He called and called but no one answered so he went all over the house looking for his mother. He even looked under the beds and behind the furnace but he couldn't find her. When he came back to the kitchen he found a piece of paper sticking in the refrigerator door. It said, "Dear Jody . . ." and then there was some more writing but Jody couldn't read it. He began to cry.

There was a knock at the back door. Jody wiped his eyes on his sleeve and opened the door. The laundry man said, "Is your mother home, Jody?"

Jody said, "Do, I dod't know what habbeded to her," and began to cry again.

The laundry man said, "Didn't she leave a note?"

Jody said, "Yes, but I cadt read id."

The laundry man said, "Let me see it."

Jody handed him the piece of paper and the laundry man read,

> "Dear Jody: I am going to the grocery store. Your medicine and your orange juice are in the refrigerator. There are sausages and toast in the oven. I'll be home in a very little while— Mother.
>
> P. S. Be sure and tell the laundry man that the laundry is in the basement."

Jody thanked the laundry man, took his medicine and ate his breakfast.

Then he went out to the treehouse but he kept forgetting which end of the hammer to use, he couldn't remember where they kept the nails, he forgot where they were going to put the window, he couldn't measure the boards because he couldn't count or read numbers so he climbed down and just sat on the grass until Julie, Jan and Linda came home.

"Hi," said Jan. "How is old dummy this morning?"

Jody said, "I'b dot a dubby."

Julie said, "Let's hear you count to ten then."

Jody said, "I'd dodt wadt to."

Julie said, "You mean you can't, dummy."

Jody said, "I'b dot a dubby."

Linda mocked him, "I'b dot a dubby. I'b dot a dubby."

Jody began to cry so the other children went in to lunch, just as Mrs. Jones came back from the store.

Seeing Jody crying under the maple tree, she asked him what the trouble was. Jody said, "The other kids tease be."

His mother said, "What do they tease you about?"

Jody said, "They call be dubby. I'b dot a dubby, ab I?"

His mother said, "I hope not, dear," and went in to fix lunch.

All afternoon Jody just sat in the sun because he couldn't think of anything to do. When the children came home from school they played Kick the Can but they didn't ask him to play, so he just watched and dozed.

At dinner the family all played What Johnny Has in His Pocket again but they didn't even try to include Jody, so after eating his dinner with his spoon, he just sat and watched the candle wax drip down the candles in the middle of the table.

After dinner Jan and Julie went up to study, Linda went to bed and Jody climbed up into his bunk and looked at the ceiling. There were two knotholes that looked just like owl's eyes. Jody looked at them until he fell asleep. At eight-thirty Mrs. Jones came in with the bottle of Ignorance Tonic but finding Jody asleep decided to wait until morning before giving him any more.

The next morning Jody woke up so very early he could hear the paper boy whistling as he threw the papers, thump, thump, thump onto each porch. Jody climbed carefully down out of his bunk, got dressed in his school clothes, went into the bathroom and washed thoroughly, brushed his teeth, combed his hair and then looked carefully at himself in the mirror. He looked just the same as always. But he certainly felt different. He felt quick and light. He tested his voice—he said, "I'm not a dummy," and it came out of his mouth, "I'm not a dummy" not "I'b dot a dubby," the way it had for the past two days. He went downstairs. It seemed very peaceful in the early morning sunlight.

Jody decided to squeeze the orange juice for his mother. He went to the cooler for the oranges and found stuck under the box the note his mother had left for him the day before. He picked it up and was surprised to find that he could read it. Every word. He began to hum a little as he cut and squeezed the oranges and poured the juice into the six glasses.

There was a gentle scratching at the back door so Jody opened it and let in Chlotilde the cat. Chlotilde rubbed against Jody's legs and purred until he stopped squeezing oranges and warmed her some milk.

When Jody had finished the oranges he decided to make some coffee. He read the directions on the can and was very pleased to see how easily he could read the hard words and fine print. He decided to make boiled coffee in the old granite picnic coffee pot. He measured the water as he filled the pot—twenty-four cups of water seemed quite a lot but Jody remembered how his mother always filled the pot at picnics. Then he measured twenty-four scoops of coffee. Then he found the coffee pot was so heavy he couldn't lift it out of the sink so he dipped out half the water into a saucepan, put the coffee pot on the stove, poured the rest in and turned the burner on high. Then he set the breakfast table, putting on a nice clean cloth.

Then he looked at the clock and found it was only just seven o'clock. He gathered up some stale bread and took it out to the squirrels. They came down out of the tree and got on his shoulder and he stood very still and watched them pick up the pieces of bread in their funny little hands and take bites out of it.

After a while Jody went back into the house to see if his coffee was boiling and was very surprised to find his mother breaking eggs into a blue bowl.

She said, "Oh, so you're the good fairy who did all this work for me. Thank you, Jody," and she hugged him.

He said, "I woke up way early, even before the paper boy."

His mother said, "How do you feel this morning?" She had noticed the neat hair, washed face and school clothes.

Jody said, "I feel just wonderful. Think I'll go to school."

His mother said, "Fine, dear, your father will be so pleased and so will Miss Robinson."

Jody said, "Miss Robinson doesn't have to worry. I'll make up my work. I'm no dummy."

His mother kissed him and said, "I should say you're not."

"Say, Mom," Jody said, "do you think I made enough coffee?" His mother looked at the enormous granite picnic coffee pot, filled clear to the brim, then at Jody's sweet anxious face. "Just right," she said. "Just exactly right. Now call the others to breakfast, dear. Tell the children to hurry or they'll be late for school."

THE WADDLE-I-DOERS

This was Saturday and the morning of the hike to the big rock. Lee woke up very early, ran into Mimi's room and jerked back the covers.

"Hey, Mimi," he said in a hoarse excited whisper. "Get up quick, this is the day we go to Big Rock to have the picnic."

Mimi turned over and opened her eyes. She said, "We can't go to the rock today because its raining."

"Oh, it is not," said Lee running to the window.

"'Tis too," said Mimi. "I woke up in the night and heard it. I was so mad I cried."

Lee pulled up the shade and sure enough, a hard spring rain was streaming down the window, pelting the bedraggled tulips and bouncing on the roof like popcorn. Lee was almost eleven but he felt like crying too because he had been counting on this hike for weeks.

So had all the other children. Mrs. Piggle-Wiggle was going to take them all to the Big Rock and they were going to walk behind the waterfall, climb up on the rock and take turns looking through Mrs. Piggle-Wiggle's very powerful spy glass, build a big bonfire and roast potatoes and weenies. They had planned to leave at six-thirty this very morning.

"Oh, how I hate rain," said Lee pounding on the window seat. "I'd just like to go out and kick it."

Mimi pulled the covers up around her chin. "I don't think I'll get up at all," she said. "It'll just be another rainy Saturday with nothing to do." She closed her eyes so Lee shuffled disconsolately back to his room and got back into bed. He lay and stared at the ceiling and listened to the pitta-patta-pitta-patta of the rain on the porch roof and hated everything and everybody in the whole world.

When his mother finally called him to breakfast, he came downstairs scowling and hitting at the furniture with his belt.

"Put on your belt, Lee dear," said his mother, "and stop snapping it at things. The buckle might scratch something."

Lee said, "Gosh, I hate rain. Why does it always have to rain on Saturday, why does it, huh, Mom?"

Mrs. Wharton said, "It does seem very unfair, I know, to have nice weather all week long and rain on Saturday, but you'll just have to learn to take the bad with the good. Where's Mimi?"

"Oh, she's not gettin' up," said Lee, picking at his egg and still scowling.

Mr. Wharton said, "As long as it's raining and you can't go on your hike, this would be a good time to clean the basement."

"Oh, Daddy!" wailed Lee. "What a horrible idea!"

"Not at all," said Mr. Wharton. "You must learn to make the best of things in this world and the best possible thing you could make of this rainy Saturday is a good job on the basement. 'Something attempted, something done, has earned a night's repose.' Now run upstairs and arouse your lazy sister."

"Now, Boyd dear," said Mrs. Wharton when Lee had left, "let's not overdo things. Remember this rainy day is a dreadful disappointment to the children and I hardly think that cleaning the basement, which is really your job, is any compensation for their disappointment."

Mr. Wharton said, "The trouble with all children today is that they are spoiled. Now when I was a boy if I got an easy job such as cleaning the basement I thought I was most fortunate. The cool dark basement seemed very pleasant to a boy who had spent hours and hours and hours hoeing cabbages in the red hot sun."

Mrs. Wharton said, "Your mother told me that from the time you were seven years old, your winters were spent in boarding school and your summers in the San Juan Islands, swimming, fishing and playing on the beach. Just when did you do all this grubbing around in a musty cellar and hoeing of cabbages in the red hot sun?"

"I spent one summer on my grandfather's farm," said Mr. Wharton stiffly, getting up from the table. "And I was only eleven years old and I worked very hard and enjoyed it. Modern children are all spoiled."

Some time after Mr. Wharton had left the house, Mimi came clumping downstairs, wearing her jeans and her mother's blue satin mules. She was as cross as two sticks and her hair looked as if she had combed it with an egg-beater.

"I hate rain," she said, grabbing a piece of toast and spreading it thickly with peanut butter.

Mrs. Wharton said, "Please put down that toast, go up-stairs and take off my best bedroom slippers, comb your hair and then say good-morning."

Mimi stuck her tongue out at Lee and clumped back up-stairs. Mrs. Wharton sighed. What a problem this day was going to be. She said to Lee, "This would be a fine day to work on your model airplane."

Lee said, "I don't wanna."

Mrs. Wharton said, "What about fixing the chain on your bicycle?"

Lee said, "I don't wanna."

Then Mimi came back, in her own shoes and combed a little, said good-morning not too sweetly, and began eat-ing her toast and peanut butter. Mrs. Wharton went out to the kitchen. Lee followed her.

He leaned against the drain-board of the sink and said, "I hate rain. Waddle I do?" His mother suggested every-thing she could think of, but he "didn't wanna" do any-thing but lean against things and say, "waddle I do?"

Pretty soon Mimi came out and leaned against Lee and said, "Waddle I do?" She didn't want to make doll clothes, she didn't want to paint, she didn't want to play games, and most of all she didn't want to wash the breakfast dishes.

Mrs. Wharton got so desperate she was just about to send Mimi up to clean the attic and Lee down to clean the basement, when the telephone rang. It was Mrs. Piggle-Wiggle and she wanted both Mimi and Lee to come over to her house right away. She said she had something very important to tell them and could they stay for lunch and dinner. Mrs. Wharton said they certainly could, in fact she would just as leave not see them again until the rain stopped. Mrs. Piggle-Wiggle laughed and said that every mother in the neighborhood felt the same way.

So Mimi and Lee put on their raincoats and galoshes and started for Mrs. Piggle-Wiggle's house. The rain blew in their faces, ran down the gutters in rivers and went glurnk, glurnk, down the drains. In front of the Burbanks, the street drain had gotten clogged with leaves and the whole street was flooded. Mimi and Lee took sticks and poked until they found the grating, then with their hands they scraped away the leaves and pretty soon the water started gurgling down the drain. The children watched it for a while then glup—it stopped. Mimi reached down and felt around. Something was stuck in the drain. She jerked and jerked and finally pulled up a large black silk scarf. It was wet and torn and she was just about to throw it away when she noticed something tied in one corner of it. She worked on the knot and Lee worked on the knot but the scarf was so wet they couldn't untie it, so they decided to carry it to Mrs. Piggle-Wiggle's and cut the knot with scissors.

When they got to Mrs. Piggle-Wiggle's all the other children were there, and there was a huge stack of galoshes and umbrellas on the porch and all the hooks in the front hall were filled with dripping raincoats. Mrs. Piggle-Wiggle opened the door for Lee and Mimi, told them to hurry and take off their things and to come into the living-room as she had something very important to tell them.

Mimi showed her the black silk handkerchief and Mrs. Piggle-Wiggle said that while Mimi was taking off her things she would take the scarf to the kitchen and cut the knot. She did and in a minute came back and handed Mimi a round gold coin. She said, "Mimi, I am quite sure that this is a pirate lucky piece. Mr. Piggle-Wiggle used to have one and as I remember it also was gold and had a skull and crossbones on it. You'd better take very good care of it. Now let's see, do you have a hanky?"

Mimi said, "No," so Mrs. Piggle-Wiggle loaned her one of hers, tied the lucky piece in the corner, put the handkerchief in Mimi's back pocket and pinned it fast with a safety pin.

"Now," said Mrs. Piggle-Wiggle, "we'll just go in the living-room with the rest of the children and perhaps later on today we'll be able to test and see if that really is a pirate's lucky piece. That certainly looked like a pirate's black silk handkerchief. I hung it up to dry in the kitchen and after a while you can iron it."

Sitting around on the floor in the living-room were Mary Lou Robertson, Kitty Wheeling, Kitty's little brother, Bobby, Bobby's friend Dicky, Hubert Prentiss, Ermintrude Bags, Gregory Moohead, Susan Grapple, Molly O'Toole, Chuckie Keystop, Dick Thompson, Patsy, Prunella Brown, Paraphernalia Grotto, Cormorant Broomrack, Bobby, Larry and Susan Gray, Catherine and Wilfred Grassfeather, Worthington and Guinevere Gardenfield,

Allen Wetherill Crankminor, Pergola Wingsproggle, Anne and Joan Russell, Jasper and Myrtle Quitrick, Sharon Rogers, Julie, Linda, Jan and Jody Jones, Wendy and Timmy Hamilton, Christopher Brown, Darsie, Bard and Alison Burbank, Armand Armadillo, Pamela, Percy and Potter Penzil, Mimi Wharton, Dicky Williams, Marilyn Matson, Benji, Stevie and Sally Franklin, Terry and Theresa Teagle. Everyone was drinking tea and eating cookies and being surly and quarrelsome in a damp rainy Saturday sort of way.

Mrs. Piggle-Wiggle sat down on a little stool by the fire-place, made room for Lightfoot the cat, Wag the dog and Lester the pig (who should have been at the Grapples' but had stayed home for the hike and picnic) by her feet, took a sip of tea, clapped her hands for quiet and began:

"I know that this horrid rain has been a great disap-pointment to all of you children—I know because I was very very disappointed myself last night when I heard rain-drops tiptoeing on the roof and tapping at the window. I also know because almost all of your mothers have told me that you children were terrible Waddle-I-Doers this morning. However, this rain and our not being able to have the picnic is actually the luckiest thing that ever hap-pened because I need all of you to help me, today, here in this house.

"You see a long, long time ago, when Mr. Piggle-Wiggle and I decided to build a house upside down, because when I was a little girl I used to lie in bed and wonder what it would be like if the house were upside down, we couldn't get anyone to build it for us because carpenters and con-tractors thought that building a house upside down was crazy, so Mr. Piggle-Wiggle built it himself. He said it wasn't too hard, he just took the plans of a regular house and used them upside down. As you all know, Mr. Piggle-Wiggle, before he retired, was a pirate and had collected quite a sizable treasure. Part of this he buried very deep somewhere in the yard, the rest of it he hid in the house, in secret cupboards and drawers.

"I didn't know anything about these secret cupboards and drawers until the house was all finished, then Mr. Piggle-Wiggle told me about them and said that there were enough secret drawers and cupboards filled with treasure to last me the rest of my life. He would not tell me where they were because he said he wanted me to experience the joy of seeking and finding treasure.

"I didn't even look for any of the treasure until after Mr. Piggle-Wiggle died. Then one day when I had used up the very last of my money, I hunted and hunted and finally found a little secret drawer filled with money. This money lasted me for almost a year. Then I hunted for and found another secret drawer with gold pieces in it. I have been doing this for ten years and have, as you know, been living very comfortably. But now I seem to have reached the end."

Mrs. Piggle-Wiggle's sweet brown eyes filled with tears but she blinked them away and went on. "You see, if it hadn't rained today we wouldn't have been able to have a picnic anyway because I used the last of the flour yesterday to make these cookies and now there is nothing at all to eat in the house. All my money has been gone for days and days and days and I have looked and looked until my eyes hurt for another secret drawer or cupboard but I can't find one. I stayed up all night long last night looking and hoping I'd find one before morning so that I could buy the supplies for our hike, but I had no luck. Of course, the money may be all gone, but I just can't believe that. I have never been extravagant and Mr. Piggle-Wiggle knew that I was very healthy and would live a long time. No, I think I've lost my feeling for secret cupboards and drawers and that is why I have asked you children to come over and help me because I know that there are no better lookers and finders in the world than children and you all know this house, how peculiarly it is built, and I'm sure that if anything was hidden in it you would find it.

"Now you must all promise me on your word of honor that you will not mention this to one soul—not even your mothers and fathers, because if word ever got around that I had money hidden in my house, the burglars would be as thick as thieves. I'm certainly hoping that you will find something before lunch but if you don't we'll just have a cup of tea and keep on looking. Fortunately I have plenty of tea and water. Now, if you don't mind, I'm going up to my room and lie down for a little. I'm very tired."

Lester got up and helped Mrs. Piggle-Wiggle to her feet, then Mrs. Piggle-Wiggle, Lester, Wag and Lightfoot went up the stairs to her room and shut the door.

For a minute or two the children just sat and looked at each other. Then Jody said, "Boy, I'll bet I can find that old money. I bet it's in the cellar." He jumped to his feet and he and Jan raced for the cellar door. Chuckie Keystop, Wilfred Grassfeather and Kitty's little brother Bobby followed.

Mary Lou Robertson said, "I think we girls should wash

the tea cups and tidy up the kitchen. Come on everybody
bring your cups to the kitchen."

Hubert Prentiss said, "I think we should organize this
search. Give everybody a certain territory and have reports."

"Oh, that's dull," said Joan Russell. "We don't want
report cards."

"I didn't say report cards, bonehead," said Hubert, "I
said reports like soldiers do."

"I think we should just stack up the cups and immediately start hunting for secret panels," said Molly
O'Toole. She put her cup and saucer in the sink and
skipped into the pantry. "The pantry's my territory,"
she said.

"I choose the dining-room," said Hubert.

"You can't have a whole room, pig," said Kitty Wheeling. "You can just have one part of the dining-room. I
dibs the buffet." She rushed through the door and put her
arms out in front of the old-fashioned built-in buffet,
which was in the wall between the kitchen and the dining-
room and arranged so that you could put dishes in the
cupboard on the kitchen side and take them out on the
dining-room side, a fact that Kitty didn't know but Hubert
did. He climbed into the lower cupboard through the
kitchen side, carefully and quietly opened the door on the
dining-room side, reached out and pinched Kitty's leg. Kitty
gave a terrible yell as though a cobra had bitten her and
Hubert laughed and said, "Oh, pardon me, I thought I had
found a cupboard of old bones."

Just then Jody came breathlessly up from the basement.
He said, "Say, did you know that Mrs. Piggle-Wiggle's

basement is flooded? The water is terrible deep and we're lookin' for the money in boats. Ole Wilfred Grassfeather was rowin' around in a dishpan and it tipped over and he looked just like an ole beaver swimmin' around with his ole beaver teeth."

Jan called from the basement, "Hey, hurry up, Jody, and bring some dry clothes for Wilfred."

Jody said, "Where will I find something dry for ole Wilfred?"

Mary Lou said, "There are some old clothes of Mr. Piggle-Wiggle's in the attic. Here, I'll get them." She ran up to the attic and got a suit of red woolen underwear out of the old trunk, then called to Wilfred to come upstairs and dry off in the bathroom.

Then she went down to the basement and told Jan and Jody to row over to the woodroom and get some wood so she could build up the fire and dry out Wilfred's clothes. The basement was certainly flooded. The water was up to the fourth step and getting higher all the time. Wilfred was dripping on the stairs and Jan and the other boys were rowing briskly around in washtubs, wash boilers and dishpans, tapping the walls and hunting for the money. Dick Thompson came down and told them to look for the basement drain but they said they were going to look for the money while the water was high and they could see up by the rafters.

By this time every child was crawling, tapping, peering, poking and feeling around in Mrs. Piggle-Wiggle's house. By noon they had found seventeen secret drawers and cupboards, all empty. Patsy found the first one. She went to pull out a drawer in the kitchen and pulled too hard and it came all the way out and lo and behold, way in behind it was another drawer. Patsy screamed with excitement and everybody came running, even Wilfred looking just like a giant firecracker in Mr. Piggle-Wiggle's long red underwear.

Then Jody came yelping up from the basement with one leg soaking wet clear to the hip, and he had found a secret cupboard in the tool bench. He just happened to lean hard on the end of the bench to keep his boat from bumping into Jan's, when the end of the tool bench came open and there was a secret cupboard, but empty. Then Molly found a little door in the ceiling of the pantry and another empty secret cupboard. Then Mary Lou found that one of the bedposts in the spare bedroom unscrewed and underneath it was a tiny drawer that pulled out, but it was empty. Then Armand Armadillo, who of course happened to be looking at the Encyclopedia, found a little sliding panel in the bookcase and when he opened it there was a tiny little cupboard, empty. Then Lee Wharton found a brick in the fireplace that came out on little hinges and behind it was a tiny drawer that pulled out, but it was empty. Paraphernalia Grotto found a board in the living-room floor that lifted up and there was a little cupboard, empty.

Mimi stood by the window, looked out at the driving rain and thought, "Everybody but me. Everybody but me is finding the secret cupboards and drawers. I'm just an old dummy. Poor Mrs. Piggle-Wiggle needs the money so much and I don't even know where to look." Tears of self-pity stung her eyelids. She reached for her handkerchief, remembered she didn't have one and wiped her eyes on the back of her hand.

"What's the matter, Mimi?" said a soft little voice.

Mimi looked down and there was Linda Jones, standing forlornly behind the curtain with her thumb in her mouth. Mimi said, "Everybody's finding the secret drawers and cupboards but me."

Linda said, "And me. Every time I find a good place to look, one of the bigger, faster children has already looked there. Anyway, I'm hungry. It must be way past lunch time."

Pergola Wingsproggle, who was sitting sadly in a chair nearby said, "It's almost two o'clock and I'm starving. Are there any cookies left?"

Mimi said, "Not one, but we can make some tea. I'll bet poor Mrs. Piggle-Wiggle would like some."

"How do you make tea," said Linda.

"Oh, you just put some tea in the pot and pour in some hot water," said Pergola, who had never made any.

"All right, then, you make it," said Mimi. "Linda and I are going to take a look at the attic."

They went up the little winding attic stairs, but Mary Lou Robertson, Anne and Joan Russell and Julie Jones were already up there poking around and arguing. "This trunk's mine," said Anne.

"No, I already chose that trunk," said Julie.

"I'm going to look in this old desk," said Joan.

"Go ahead," said Mary Lou, "Dick Thompson and Gregory Moohead already almost tore it apart."

"Oh, boy, I'm going to look in this old toy box," said Linda.

"People don't hide money in toy boxes," said Anne.

"I do," said Linda. "I hid twenty-five cents in my toy box last Christmas."

Mimi went over and stood by the chimney. It was warm and she felt cold, a little damp and very sad. "Ouch," —something stuck her. She felt her back pocket and found the safety pin pinning Mrs. Piggle-Wiggle's handkerchief in her pocket had come undone. Mimi tried to fasten it but it wouldn't fasten. It seemed to be broken. She took it off and threw it away. Then suddenly the wind gave a big howl and the lights went off. It wasn't dark outside but it was completely dark in the attic, except for a little bit of milky daylight that squeezed in through the one small cobwebby window.

The children all began scrambling around, bumping into each other and the furniture trying to find the stairway. Little Linda Jones fell over the toy box she had just been searching through and began to bawl. "Somebody pushed me. There's a ghost up here."

Mimi said, "Don't be silly, Linda. The lights were on just a second ago and there wasn't any ghost up here. Here, give me your hand."

But as she bent over to help Linda her jeans caught on a loose board back of the chimney and suddenly she was as scared and panicky as Linda. She knew that it was only a loose board that snagged her back pocket, but in the darkness it felt like a strong bony hand. Everything else up in the attic seemed to have changed too. The big old-fashioned dresser now looked like a great monster with paws raised ready to pounce; Mr. Piggle-Wiggle's shabby old trunk looked like a coffin; the old broken rocking-chair looked like a witch kneeling by her cauldron; the desk looked like the opening to a big cave. Mimi jerked her pocket off the board and she and Linda stumbled across the attic and down the stairs.

Down in the living-room, Mrs. Piggle-Wiggle was lighting big fat white plumber's candles and distributing them to the older children. "Be careful," she warned each one. "Don't put your candle down—just give it to someone to hold for you. Has anyone had any luck yet?"

"I did," yelled Patsy. "I found a secret drawer, but it was empty." The other children all told her of their finds, but added every time, "it was empty."

Mrs. Piggle-Wiggle said, "Don't worry about finding only empty secret cupboards and drawers. The important thing is that you found them. That your eyes and ears are so sharp that you found in a few hours what it has taken me ten years to find. Now everybody get busy. I just know we're going to find a new secret cupboard before the lights go on again. Isn't it fun to hunt for secrets in the dark? Aren't you glad there's a storm?"

The children all said yes in scary hushed voices, took their candles and again began to search.

Mimi was the last to get a candle and when Mrs. Piggle-Wiggle handed it to her she said, "Hasn't your lucky piece helped you find the secret yet, Mimi?"

Mimi said, "Oh, no, Mrs. Piggle-Wiggle. I'm just terribly dumb about finding things. I've looked and looked and I haven't even found one secret cupboard."

Mrs. Piggle-Wiggle said, "Take out your lucky piece and rub it hard between your thumb and first finger. We'll just see if it really is a real Pirate's lucky piece."

Mimi reached in her back pocket but Mrs. Piggle-Wiggle's hanky with the lucky piece tied in the corner was gone. She reached in the other pocket. It wasn't there either. She said, "It's gone, Mrs. Piggle-Wiggle. I've lost it."

Then she remembered how she had caught her pocket on the board behind the chimney in the attic. She said, "I think I know where it is, though. I think I left it up in the attic."

Mrs. Piggle-Wiggle said, "Do you want me to go up with you?"

Mimi did but she didn't want to admit that she was afraid, so she said, "Oh, no, I'll take my candle and go up, I know just where to look."

She ran up the stairs and to the door to the attic so fast, her candle flame leaned way over to one side and threatened to go out. Mrs. Piggle-Wiggle called to her, "Better take some extra matches, Mimi; it's draughty in the attic. There are some on that little shelf there by the landing." Mimi grabbed a handful of the matches and then started slowly up the attic stairs.

Her candle flame grew very high as if it were trying to peer over the stairway, then ducked down as a sudden gust of cold air flew at them from under the eaves. The sounds of the storm were much clearer up here. The wind moaned and whined around the eaves and the rain lashed furiously at the window and hammered hard on the roof, demanding to get in. Mimi held the candle high and looked around. There was the trunk, there was the rocking-chair, there was the toy box, and there was a terrible monster, oh, no, the bureau.

She picked her way over to the chimney. Ooh, it was dark over there. A gust of wind blew her candle out. It was a big gust of wind, almost like an open window. Mimi hurriedly struck one of the matches—it blew out, too. She struck another—it also blew out. Another and another. Finally she had only two left. With trembling fingers she lit the next to last one. The flame held and the candle sputtered and then flared cozily.

Mimi bent over and peered behind the chimney. There was the board and there hanging to a corner of it was Mrs. Piggle-Wiggle's handkerchief. Mimi reached for it but it seemed to be caught on something. She jerked hard and slowly a big piece of the attic wall opened. Mimi held her candle higher so she could see better. Behind the piece of wall, which was hinged like a little door, there were six drawers with little handles. Mimi opened one. It was stuffed full of green paper money. Mimi opened another —it was filled with gold pieces. She opened another—it was filled with silver; another held jewels; another held more paper money; another more gold.

Mimi rushed to the stairway and yelled, "Mrs. Piggle-Wiggle, Mrs. Piggle-Wiggle, I've found it! I've found it! Money! Jewels! Hurry!"

Everyone came running but the first to poke his head over the attic stairway was Lester. Mimi knelt down and hugged him. "Oh, Lester, dear!" she said, "Mrs. Piggle-Wiggle's rich. Isn't it wonderful?"

Lester smiled.

When Mrs. Piggle-Wiggle came up she walked over to the secret cupboard and just stood with her arm around Mimi and with tears streaming from her eyes. Mimi opened the drawers one by one and Mrs. Piggle-Wiggle looked at the treasure and wiped her eyes. "Dear Mr. Piggle-Wiggle," she said. "I knew he wouldn't forget me. I just knew it."

As each one of the children had to see the cupboard and examine the treasure, hear over and over exactly how Mimi had found it, and see and feel the wonderful magic lucky piece, it was dark before they finally went downstairs. Then Mrs. Piggle-Wiggle said, "My goodness, how selfish I've been. Here you poor children are all hungry and I've been so excited over the treasure I forgot all about dinner. What do you say we have our picnic after all—we'll roast potatoes and weenies in the fireplace, we'll get chocolate ice cream and I'll bake a cake to celebrate. Now first I'll go to the store and while I'm gone you boys can row to the woodroom and get a lot of wood so we can have a nice roaring fire. And Dick, would you please go down and see if you can find the basement drain? Mimi, you and Mary Lou and Kitty come to the store and help me carry the groceries, and you Molly and Hubert see that everyone has on dry clothes and that the house is picked up a little."

Just then the lights went on. "Hooray, hooray!" shouted everyone but Jody and Lee. They said, "Oh, darn the ole lights. It was lots more fun down in the basement rowing around with candles. We pretended we were in a flooded mine and we used our candles to test the air for oxygen."

"When you go down again, use your paddles to test the floor for a drain," said Mrs. Piggle-Wiggle, laughing.

Just then Dick Thompson came running up from the basement. He said, "Say, Mrs. Piggle-Wiggle, I found the drain and there was something over it and so I scraped it off with this stick and look, it seems to be a letter to you."

Mrs. Piggle-Wiggle took the soggy piece of paper and read:

> "Dear Wife:
> My last secret cupboard is very hard to find so I am leaving this letter on your gardening shelf in the basement as I am sure that before too many years this shelf will become so crowded and cluttered you will have to clean it off and then you will find this letter. The last secret cupboard of treasure is behind the chimney in the attic. Just jerk hard on that old loose board.
>   Your loving husband,
>   Mr. Piggle-Wiggle"

"Well, for heaven's sake," said Mrs. Piggle-Wiggle. "I looked on that gardening shelf last night and I remember when that letter fell to the floor. I thought it was an old empty seed package and didn't bother to pick it up. I never would have found it if it hadn't been for you, Dick, and I never would have found the secret drawers. This rain certainly has brought us luck. It clogged the drain by the Burbanks' so Mimi would find the pirate's lucky piece and it clogged the drain in my cellar so I would find Mr. Piggle-Wiggle's letter. I guess from now on I'll always have to like rain, even on picnic days."

The End

ABOUT THE AUTHOR

BETTY MACDONALD was born in Boulder, Colorado, and grew up in various places in the West. As a child her activities included singing, ballet, piano, French, dramatics, cooking, shooting, and roof-painting. She attended Roosevelt High School in Seattle and the University of Washington.

Ms. MacDonald worked at an assortment of jobs: as secretary to a mining engineer, tinting photographs, keeping records for a rabbit grower, running a chain letter office, modeling fur coats, and selling advertising. She also did government work, which included teaching art and writing.

She was married twice, first to a chicken farmer named Robert Haskett (her successful book THE EGG AND I was based on reminiscences of their experiences on the farm) and then to Donald MacDonald. The Mrs. Piggle-Wiggle stories were first told to her daughters, Anne and Joan. Ms. MacDonald died in 1958.